The Dictator's Astrologer

Roberleigh H Claigh

The Dictator's Astrologer

Helm Publishing

For information address:
Helm Publishing
3923 Seward Ave.
Rockford, IL 61108
815-398-4660
www.publishersdrive.com

ISBN 978-0-9792328-9-3

Printed in the United States of America

AUTHOR'S NOTE

Although *The Astrologer's Dictator* is based on the life of Afra Waesch, an astrologer in Nazi Germany, it's a work of fiction. With the exception of some of the dialogue the historical events are authentic, as are occurrences such as Hitler's dealings with Satanist Dietrich Eckart, Hitler claiming the Spear of Destiny, his occult hideaway in the Bavarian Alps, the Nazi Occult Bureau, Britain's astrological espionage, the astrological plot that enabled the British to capture Hitler's deputy, Rudolph Hess, and the Americans discovering a hidden cache of treasures including the Spear of Destiny after the war. Afra did have a guardian angel.

Acknowledgements

Thank you my dear husband and good friend, Dr. Grady Deal, PhD, LMT, DC who has helped me with all my projects for twenty-seven years. He helped edit this book and my other books, suggested ideas, worked out computer problems and has been generally helpful and kind. I am blessed.

I am very grateful for two highly gifted editors and authors, Loretta Anawalt and Katrina St. Marie, who inspired me and contributed so much to my book. Thank you JoAnn Lordahl and her writers' group: Miriam Pearson, Petra Sundheim, Lisette Langlois, Ruthie Lewis and Edie Seymour. To Hilary who opened my eyes to a higher vision. To master astrologer, Kathleen Herron for good suggestions.

Afra's best friend, Coni Wesland recommended that I write this book. She shared many insights into Afra and her two daughters, Ellen and Lilo. Yvonne, Ellen's close friend contributed much about cabaret life during that period.

PROLOGUE

Vienna – Twenty year old Adolph Hitler was on the sidewalk working on a drawing. Suddenly the sky darkened. The first winter wind drove icy rain in his face. His sketchbook was sodden, his drawing ruined. It was a moment of anger mixed with painful self-knowledge. The Vienna Academy of Fine Arts had turned him down. To them, he was a miserable failure, his grand ambitions worthless.

The first winter wind whipped around, tore his sketchbook from his hands and flung it to the ground. He thrust his pencils in his pocket and stomped over to retrieve it. An explosion of thunder and flash of lightning stunned him as the darkening sky opened and drenched him with driving rain. His ruined drawing lay in a ditch.

Seeking shelter, he ran to the subject of his drawing, Hapsburg Treasure House, and pushed open the heavy doors. He could still hear the heavy beat of the rain, but he stood miserably, his wet clothes dripping onto his shoes. He left the vestibule and entered the spacious untended hall, so despondent he scarcely noticed the beautiful crowns, scepters and ornate regalia surrounding him. He wandered aimlessly down the aisles, pausing before a display, barely aware of the glass-encased artifacts.

A group of foreigners stopped nearby, taken aback by the wet shabby figure with uncut hair and gaunt, hungry eyes. Their guide brought their attention to an iron Spearhead, black with age. "Associated with this ancient talisman of power is a legend of two opposing forces, light and darkness. Whoever claims the Spear of Destiny and unravels its secrets holds the destiny of the world in his hands -- for good or evil."

Fascinated by inherent instincts of tyranny and conquest, Hitler listened with fixed attention.

"This legend," explained the guide, "originated at the time of the Crucifixion of Jesus, the Christ. Gaius Cassius, a Roman centurion filled with compassion, spurred his horse and charged toward the Cross. He plunged the Spear into Jesus' side to shorten his suffering. The sun eclipsed. The world fell into darkness. A storm broke, thunder crashed, rain pelted the earth. Cassius dropped to his knees and bowed his head, worshipping before the body of Jesus that shone with holy light in the darkness. In that moment Cassius's heart opened to the revelation of Christ, who was giving his life to redeem mankind."

The guide's words aroused Hitler. He studied the ancient artifact lying in an open leather case on a faded red velvet cushion. Its point was secured in a wide base with metal flanges depicting the wings of a dove. Embossed on the hilt were three golden crosses. As he focused on the Spearhead he sensed something emanating from it – a hidden power he couldn't identify.

The next day, he began a diligent search at the Hof Library. Tracing the Spear through the centuries, he studied the lives of the men who had claimed it as their possession. Forty-five emperors, including Charlemagne, the first Holy Roman Emperor, professed to wield its powers.

Hitler's imagination was most excited by the great German Frederick Barbarossa and his grandson, Frederick the Second. Frederick Barbarossa had conquered Italy. Frederick the Second was a notable statesman, a skillful and courageous commander, a gifted occultist who believed in astrology and practiced alchemy. Prizing the Spear above all things, he called on its powers during his Crusades and throughout his battles with the Italian States and Papal Armies.

As Hitler examined the glorious history of the Spearhead, the hopelessness of his own life bore down on him like a stone. He loathed being a nonentity, a failure, a bum roaming the streets.

He was determined to unravel the Spear's secrets and harness its powers. When he stood once again before the ancient weapon, surrounding sounds at the Treasure House melted away. The air became stifling. He could hardly breathe. Hovering above the Spear he made out a misty form, a Dark Spirit, sardonic and cruel. Had Hitler been a different person he might have been repelled; he might have been aware of the opposing Spirit inherent in the Spear, a holy force of the radiance, love and compassion of Christ. Instead, desolately consumed with fear, he drew the Spirit of black magical powers to him.

"I put myself in your hands," he said to the frightening figure before him. "Do with me what you will."

A mocking smile formed on the apparition's lips.

Filled with conflicting feelings of both hope and terror, Hitler left the Treasure House.

Thirty years later he went back to the Museum to claim the Spear of Destiny for himself. At last he thought, the power is truly mine.

Chapter 1

Kassel, Germany 1914 – "Father, I have to go!" seventeen year old Afra wailed as she leapt out of her chair. "How can you do this? You know how hard I've studied!"

"Afra," her mother interrupted, "don't talk to your father that way. Have you no respect? Do you really think he wants to disappoint you?"

Afra dropped back into her chair, seething with resentment. She'd dreamed of the day when she'd go to the university. Blessed with fine intellectual ability, she was driven to attain knowledge and understand more deeply. Above all else, she wanted to be a writer. As a child she had a notebook in which she wrote her observations, ideas and made-up stories. For some reason, she wanted to see her words in tangible form. It seemed to her as though spoken thoughts just drifted away in the atmosphere.

Her father hated to put restrictions on his daughter, but he had no choice. "We know how much you want to go to the university." At the eager look on her face, he steeled himself for what he had to say. "But now that I've been drafted we have to cut back on expenses. Listen to me. Germany has the best-drilled armies in the world. The war will be over quickly. We will be the victor. Germany has always been strong and prestigious, a warrior country respected by everyone." He quickly added, "After we win the war we should be able to afford the university. For the present I'm afraid it will be more practical for you to attend business trade school."

And when will the war be over? Afra agonized. It could be years before that happened. She struggled to control her anger. No matter what, she was determined she'd never lose sight of her goal.

Nevertheless, her family's financial situation made it imperative that she get a job as soon as she graduated from trade school. She was hired by a women's labor union, a new concept in the world. She negotiated work and salary terms for office workers and store clerks. The repetitive routine, restraints and limited horizons of office work galled her. She was ambitious and still longed for the day when she could devote her time to writing. Will I be stuck in this job forever? Afra wondered.

Nobody dreamed the war would drag on for over four years. It began with Britain, France, Russia, Germany and Austria-Hungary, and over time escalated into a world war. It involved soldiers from five different continents. Approximately nine million young men were killed.

1918 -- When Afra's father returned after Germany's defeat, his eyes were haunted by the horrors he'd experienced. "I thought I'd left it all behind me when I came home," he said to his wife Elise and Afra. "But today in Kassel I saw wounded veterans begging on the street corners. The next thing I knew I was walking on shattered glass in front of a ransacked butcher shop." His voice took on an edge of anger. "Food is so scarce any store displaying it is a target for the hungry. It's depressing to see my family with barely enough to eat. Our economy is ruined, and politically the country is in shambles."

Afra, too, was not happy with her job. "Herr Dietrich," she said to an unremarkable looking man sitting by her desk, "you'll be comfortable in this job. You have an aptitude for it."

"Thank you, Fraulein Moehlhendrich." He unfolded his cap as he stood up, and left the office slapping it against his thigh with satisfaction.

She should have been pleased, yet it annoyed her to see him so cheerful while she felt such discontent.

Nearby Suse, her friend and co-worker, flipped back her strawberry blond hair as she laughed and joked with a client. Suse made Afra feel plain and introverted. Not only was she high spirited and outgoing, she was also glamorous. One of Suse's greatest pleasures was shopping. She had a colorful, pretty wardrobe.

Clothes bored Afra; she preferred dressing conservatively and comfortably. What fascinated her was the human mind; she was in awe of scholars and brilliant people.

"Look at the clock, will you?" said Suse, turning to Afra. "Are you ready for lunch?"

"Yes. Let's get out of here." They picked up their purses and lunch baskets and headed for the park. The beautiful, sunny day awakened Afra's innate optimism. Today, she thought, anything could happen.

Their favorite bench was unoccupied. They sat and unwrapped their sandwiches. People milled about – walkers, bicyclists, a mother pushing a baby carriage. They talked about Germany's political situation, of concern to everyone. Unlike the Imperial regime, the new democratic process was slow-moving. "There are so many new parties springing up," said Afra. "The Social Democratic Party. The Christian Democratic Party. The Communist Party. And the tiny German Workers' Party. They all have different plans so it's hard to know which group, if any, is best."

Suse thought it over. "One party I definitely don't care for is the Communists; they want only to provoke a revolution. Thank God ex-soldiers in the Free Corps crushed two of their uprisings."

"I don't like the Communists either. You'd think by now people would want to find more peaceful ways of settling disputes."

"Oh sure!" countered Suse. "See what happened when our so-called Republican Government buckled under and signed the Peace Treaty! Outrageous terms! Nothing has changed."

"Alright!" Afra flung her hands up, annoyed by all the complaints she'd heard about the Peace Treaty. "Let's get on with it. We need someone with a solution to our economic problems!"

"And I suppose you, the expert, know the answer."

"Hello Suse!" a voice broke in, a tall lean man, his jacket flung over his shoulder.

He was the most handsome man Afra had ever seen, rugged and masculine yet with an intelligent face and dark brown eyes that pierced right through her.

"Oh, hello," said Suse. "This is my friend, Afra Moehlhendrich," She turned to her. "Afra, Hagan Waesch."

"Glad to meet you, Fraulein," he said as he made a small bow. He observed her more closely. Her modest dress of pleated cotton with white buttons and collar failed to conceal a curvaceous figure and long, slim legs. Although she wasn't a beautiful woman, there was something about her – a kind of self-assurance, as though she knew who she was and where she was going. What piqued his interest most was the contrast between her outer reserve and the smoldering passion of her tawny eyes. His expression took on a wicked glint of humor. "And what is your opinion of the political situation, Fraulein Moelhendrich?"

"In my opinion, Herr Waesch, none of the parties has a clear idea of what they want or how they're going to get it. There's a terrible lack of talent, of real leadership."

"Ah, I see you're a woman with a mind of your own. And I absolutely agree with you. The strikes, gun fights and demonstrations in the streets are upsetting to say the least."

"It's discouraging," Afra replied. "But surely something better will come from it all." Their eyes met and she could feel an intense attraction between them. It took her by surprise. Most men were usually put off by her reserve. Perhaps that's why his utter masculinity and obvious interest sent adrenaline charging through her blood. Flustered, she broke her gaze and glanced at her watch. "We'll be late, Suse."

He wasn't deterred. "May I call you?"

"So Afra, what do you think about Herr Waesch?" asked Suse on their way back to the office. "He's obviously taken with you."

"Oh Suse, I just met him."

Why did she feel so inhibited? She knew she appeared reticent and standoffish. Somehow it was impossible to express the jumble of strong feelings that often raced inside her -- sexual attraction, passion, love, anger, frustration. She didn't have an easy manner that appealed to men. It would be nice to have a boyfriend, but what chance did she have with so many flirtatious girls around? She looked at Suse and shook her head. "Anyway, he probably won't call."

"Of course he will."

Afra looked at her friend, surprised by her assured tone.

"I'm a pretty good judge of men, Afra. He's attracted to you. He sees you as a challenge. He knows if he can open you up, he'll find a treasure."

Chapter 2

Alone in her room, Afra felt trapped in her dead-end job. She thought about Hagan, wondering what it would be like to be kissed by him. What would it be like if they became lovers? If she met him again she'd be different. She'd give him a big smile and look right into his eyes. The sharp ring of the phone cut her short. She knew it was Hagan. She ran to the phone, "Hello?"

"Hello, Afra?"

Her heart jumped.

"I thought we might have a bite to eat at Gutsschanke Neuhof and then go to a movie."

"I'd like that," Afra replied. "Gutsschanke Neuhof is a favorite place of mine."

When they arrived at the garden restaurant the sun was beginning to set. They decided to eat on the terrace under a leafy tree. Almost at once a pretty waitress appeared at their side. "Let me give you a couple of menus," she said, dimples appearing on her cheeks. After a careful perusal, they opted for the venison accompanied by bread made on the premises and wine from the owner's vineyard.

After the waitress left, Hagan pulled a pipe and matches from his pocket. He lit up and inhaled a satisfying stream of air and smoke.

"So Hagan," Afra said, "Suse tells me you're a journalist."

"Yes, I am," he answered, as he laid down his pipe. "And, like many journalists, I've always wanted to write a book. I just finished my first effort, *A Tail Gunner's Tale.*"

"Catchy title," Afra remarked. "Were you a tail gunner during the war?"

"No, I was very lucky to have been a pilot instead of down in the trenches." He leaned in to her and spoke intently. "Nothing since has equaled the exhilaration of flying in the vastness of the sky." His eyes had a faraway look.

"I've heard about the aerial dogfights," said Afra breaking into his thoughts. "Weren't they scary?"

"Oh yes!" He was with her again. "But the chases and battles with British and American pilots were also incredibly exciting! We were living on the edge, never knowing what the next moment would bring. Once we were high above the clouds, when we spotted two English aircraft. We attacked with guns flaming! We had a hit! And then another! Both planes plummeted into the clouds, fire streaming behind them. We followed and saw them plow into the earth. Good riddance!"

Afra's eyes glowed with the excitement of the battle, of soaring through an endless sky. And here she was, sitting next to one of Germany's great heroes! Then unbidden, her imagination swept her away to a scene of being married to Hagan. How wonderful it would be to have the love and companionship of marriage and a family.

Abruptly she was brought back to reality when she noticed his eyes slide toward their waitress as she approached and deftly set their order on the table. Was it the same appraisal he'd given her at the park? She looked down at her plate, feeling a rush of jealousy, berating herself for being upset about a man she hardly knew.

"I haven't seen you here before," Hagan said to the waitress, noting her curvaceous figure, basking in the flirtatious cast to her eyes.

"My parents and I just moved here from Hagen."

"What a coincidence. My name is Hagan," he grinned.

"Hmm." She tucked a curl behind her ear, her hand beautifully manicured with rose colored nail polish. "You'll both enjoy the venison," she said and walked away.

Hagan sipped his wine, the waitress quickly forgotten. He thought how different Afra was from most of the women he'd encountered. There was nothing coy or teasing about her. That made her all the more interesting. There was a lot more to her than a sly enticing look.

"Let me tell you something else that lingers in my memory," he said. "We were flying over the front lines when we saw one of our brass bands playing a concert for our men. Even more remarkably, American soldiers had crossed no man's land and were lying on the ground by our barbed wire listening to the music. Such a peaceful moment amidst a terrible war." For a moment stillness pervaded his being. He laid his pipe on the table with a sigh and held her in his gaze. "But now, my reserved new friend, something is different. I can't explain it. Somehow life has new meaning."

Afra had the same feeling. It wasn't just his heroics as a pilot. She was much more touched by his tale of the Germans and Americans listening to the band. He'd flown high while she was earthbound. She began to relax, caught in the spell of his stories. There was a side to him that longed for freedom and wide-open spaces. Did he feel confined as she did by the boundaries they all felt since Germany's terrible defeat?

The food was superb, but she was so filled with anticipation she'd lost her appetite.

"Do you know, Afra, even though we've just met, I seem to spend all my time waiting to be with you again."

"I do too." The words slipped out, and she felt her face flush with heat.

Hagan was amused. "I have an idea something is going on." He took hold of her hand.

Afra felt it, too, but she pressed her elbows to her sides. Hagan saw her uneasiness and withdrew his hand. "Anyway," he tactfully changed the subject, "I do have another diversion. I usually go running four or five times a week"

She smiled. "I noticed that you move with the ease of an athlete."

"Did you? I'm glad you noticed." He looked at her with dark, seductive eyes.

The movie was a lighthearted romance filled with beautiful people. It ended with the lovers in each other's arms. The pianist, watching from the front of the theater, played a dreamy melody. The lovers' faces drew together in a kiss. The lights came on. The pianist segued into an upbeat tune while everyone filed out. For Afra, the best part of the evening was seeing Hagan again, feeling his arm on her shoulder and his warm hand on her arm, every cell in her body alive.

They strolled down the quiet street. It was a magical night. Stars streamed through the sky and a full moon glided over the buildings.

"That moon reminds me of you, Afra. There's a secret part of you as remote and mysterious as the moon." Being a curious man, he found that exciting. He wanted to be allowed behind her walls. He took her hand and drew her close. Her free hand was gripped into a tight fist, caught in conflict between withholding and out-rushing desire. Before she could figure out why she was resisting, he cradled her in his arms and kissed her. "Afra," he whispered. At first she didn't respond. Then his kiss and the feel of his lean hard body overwhelmed her. Her face was flushed, her heart racing wildly.

The moment was shattered by a group of noisy people bursting from a nearby restaurant. The moon slipped behind a building, its spell broken. Reluctantly he let her go.

A week later, Afra gazed in her bedroom mirror, pleased. As a rule she was unimpressed by fancy clothes, but yesterday she'd bought a dress that was distinctively red. In it she felt like a butterfly coming out of a cocoon. It heightened the color of her cheeks, its slim waist and flowing skirt emphasized her figure. She ran her hands over the skirt, the soft folds moving her imagination. The doorbell rang -- Hagan, right on time for their dinner date.

"The night is young, Afra," he said, leading her to his automobile. "Let's go for a couple of beers and a bite to eat."

They drove to Muller's Tavern, a friendly place filled with people huddled over foaming tankards of beer, engaged in ribald conversation and beer drinking songs. They made their way to a table by an open fireplace.

"You look wonderful in that dress," Hagan complimented her after ordering. The flames from the fire gave her cheeks a radiant glow.

"Thank you, Hagan," She met his eyes. It was the closest she could come to shaking the reticence she experienced around eligible men.

He broke into her thoughts, "The last time we were out I talked about nothing but me. Tell me, how do you like your job at the Labor Union?"

"Oh, it's all right," she replied. "I suppose I'm lucky to be working during these difficult times, but I find the work boring and unchallenging."

He wasn't surprised. He could tell she had a sharp brain. "What kind of work would you like to be doing?"

She told him of her dreams that someday, somehow she'd be able to go to the university. His concern made her feel even closer to him. Still, she concluded her story quickly. Why spoil the evening going over her problems when they could enjoy each other's company in such a happy, convivial place?

~~

Munich, September 12, 1919 -- That same evening, the German Workers' Party held a meeting in the shabby, dimly lit back room of a rundown tavern in Munich. A waitress circulated among a small group of rowdy beer drinkers sitting on hard backed chairs lined up at a table. Mostly working class men, they wore sweaters and breeches with coarse woolen stockings, their caps resting on their laps. They fidgeted, half listening to Professor Baumann, the evening's speaker, half savoring their foamy beer.

In monotonous tones Baumann advocated Bavarian succession from Germany.

A strident angry voice cut him short. "That's idiotic! That's treason!" A short fellow with dark hair falling across his forehead jumped up from his chair. "How can you even suggest such a stupid idea?" he shouted.

The astonished audience stared at him. At last things were livening up.

"Germany has to remain united!" The man flung his fist up in defiance. "It's the *only* way for her to return to greatness." He expanded on his ideas, and then abruptly sat down with a smug look. Galvanized by his fervent speech, the little group pounded their mugs on the table, their voices raised in agreement.

When the noise died down someone in the audience called out, "And what is your name, sir?"

"Adolph Hitler," came the reply in a tone of supreme self-confidence.

He leaned back in his chair totally at ease. Inside his mind was racing. This is my chance, he thought. The top echelon of the Thule Society, that is myself, Dietrich Eckart, Heinrich Himmler, Rudolph Hess and Alfred Rosenberg, is becoming more political. Our plan is to bring the German Workers' Party under our leadership.

Chapter 3

"Come in, Afra," her father commanded. She slowly opened the parlor door.

"You wanted to see me?"

"Yes. Your mother and I would like to talk to you." He paced back and forth with heavy strides, his brows creased. Her mother sat quietly, her hands clasped in her lap.

Afra sat down, all attention. "Afra, we understand why you're so attracted to Hagan," her father began. "He has a likeable personality. He's smart, well-informed on a variety of subjects and will probably be successful in life. But Afra," he spoke with the bearing of one who's sure of his opinion, "we don't trust him."

She frowned. Before she could speak, her mother began. "There's something about Hagan that's hard for me to put my finger on. It's as though there are times when he unexpectedly changes. He seems to be ardently in love with you. Nevertheless, I think he's the kind of man who will always see the grass as being greener on the other side of the fence. It's so easy to be misled by outer appearances and emotions," her mother implored.

Her father nodded. "She's right. Passionate feelings can carry anyone away, but passion doesn't necessarily mean love."

Her mother went on, "Please Afra, think about this. Passion is such an overwhelming emotion it can totally obscure reason." She leaned forward to emphasize her point. "We know you're stable. Still, sometimes you can be very stubborn, charging into things without thinking them through."

Her father's back was up. "Remember, and remember well, that when you get married you'll be tied to that person the rest of your life."

Afra burst out in frustration, "I understand you want what's best for me, but in no way do I agree with you!" She rose from her chair. "You think you know Hagan, but you don't! You don't know him at all!" Her body was stiff with indignation. "What all of this comes down to is that you're asking me to break off with him. I don't think I could bear to do that." She tried to swallow her stinging tears. "First I had to give up my hopes of going to the university. Now I'm supposed to give up Hagan!" Never before had she spoken to her parents that way, but it seemed as though she was blocked at every turn.

"Afra, Afra!" her mother cried, aware that her daughter could be unreasonable once she made up her mind. "Please be patient. You haven't known Hagan long enough. Wait a year before you make any decisions that could change your life, irrevocably."

"I will think about your advice. Please excuse me. I'm going to bed now." She needed time alone to process her feelings. Dutifully she bade them goodnight. As she turned to go, her knee banged into the coffee table. Steeling herself, she made it to the other side of the door before grappling with the pain. It wasn't just her knee that hurt. She felt crushed by the weight of her parents' words. What if they were right and she couldn't trust her heart? Though she felt an overwhelming passion for Hagan, she knew there was much more to their relationship. She loved him deeply, dreamed of their being together forever. She made her way up the stairway and down the hall to her bedroom. Closing the door behind her, she sat on her bed crying as though her heart was torn in two.

That night she prayed. She deliberated over everything her parents had said. But in truth, she was sure she was right about Hagan. What did her parents know?

Three months later, the minister concluded, "For better or worse, through sickness and health, I now pronounce you man and wife." Hagan looked at Afra, and for a moment he saw the beautiful smile of a woman looking into the eyes of her man. He took her in his arms and kissed her so ardently she felt a wave of love and passion flood through her body. She was married to the man of her dreams. A whole wonderful life was opening up.

The next year Lilo was born. Baby Ellen came the following year. Hagan's book was published along with the recovering economy, and he had a contract to write another. Although everything should have been perfect, Afra was becoming aware of conflicting desires within herself. On one hand, she was incredibly happy being a wife and mother. On the other, she was still ambitious and often felt frustrated held down to housewifery duties. Although she tried to spend some time writing, it was difficult with two lively little children demanding her attention.

~~

During this period Hitler was disgusted over the Versailles Treaty and postwar problems. Motivated by ambition and a strong sense of public consciousness, he decided to go into politics. At first he hadn't been impressed by the German Workers' Party. Yet there was something about those shabby men that appealed to him: their longing for a new movement that would be more than a party in the former sense of the word. Also, and certainly not to be overlooked, the unimportance of the organization would make it easier to use as a springboard for his ambitions. After carefully pondering the matter, he decided to join.

Above everything else, he was driven to gain recognition, authority and power. Although he hated tedious menial work, he wasted no time. He prodded the timid committee to organize bigger meetings. He typed invitations and distributed them. He increased their number by having them mimeographed. But when he personally delivered eighty of them only seven people came. He refused to give up and placed a notice in the local newspaper. This time one hundred and eleven people came.

The drudgework finally began to pay off. "We want you to follow the main speaker with a fifteen minute closing talk," he was told. However, Hitler always did things his way, and his lengthy and inflammatory oratory brought in three hundred marks. He was becoming a popular and the meetings continued to grow. At last he spoke before an audience of two thousand people. The applause was deafening!

He renamed the party the National Socialist Party.

~~~

Occasionally Afra needed to get out. Visits to her mother were precious. They'd sit in Mutti's kitchen drinking tea. Afra loved talking about Ellen and Lilo, and Mutti occasionally slipped in a piece of motherly advice. "Afra, I know that sometimes you're a bit overbearing, but there are also times when you don't stand up for yourself."

"What do you mean?" asked Afra, hating to be criticized

"Last week when you were here with the children, Lilo threw a fit because you didn't bring her playthings. You were angry and retreated into yourself for the rest of the afternoon. Afra, I know you try to avoid arguments, but when something is bothering you it's always best to talk it over calmly." She patted her daughter's hand. "Otherwise, resentment only builds up over the years – like shoving dirt under the carpet."

Afra stifled a sigh. Her mother was right. Her emotions were dangerous. If she let them out she'd explode. To keep the peace
~~~

she had to repress them. It wasn't only her. Lilo could be difficult at times.

And Hagan was so temperamental she had to watch every word lest he took things the wrong way. It was a hard lesson for her to learn to be less blunt and more diplomatic. Their marriage had gradually become a mess. They never talked things over any more. They both stewed and fought but nothing changed.

~~

October, 1929 – For some time Hitler had been predicting disaster. Now a World Depression cast its shadow over Germany. Gradually unemployment reached the six million mark. Hundreds of thousands of people stood hopeless in bread lines. Everyone was suffering from widespread inflation. Wages were worthless, purchasing power nil.

Afra's situation was dismal. Like everyone else she was having a hard time making ends meet. Hagan put in long hours working due to their sudden shortage of money.

Hitler and the National Socialists, called Nazis for short, were quick to take advantage of these circumstances with unremitting attacks on the parliamentary republic and democratic methods of government.

Afra wondered if their interest in the economy was only for their own political advancement.

~~

"Afra, come over here," her next-door neighbor Hazel called from the fence that separated their properties.

Although Hazel was a bit of a gossip, Afra enjoyed chatting with her when she had a spare moment.

"You haven't seen my cat around, have you?"

"No, I haven't. But I've been busy in the house. She could be sitting on our front porch for all I know."

"Oh well," she'll probably show up sooner or later. Hazel leaned over the fence, anticipating a chance to pass on some gossip. "Afra," she lowered her voice, "I thought I should tell you. The other night Stark and I were out, and I happened to see Hagan and some woman together."

Afra managed to hide her alarm behind a straight face. "Hazel, it was just an old friend of ours. They went to the store for me to pick up some salt." She stepped back from the fence. "I'm in kind of a hurry right now. I'll talk to you later."

The minute she was inside she ran to the bedroom and curled up on the bed, jealous and sick at heart. Tears of distress washed down her face. She sulked in anger and biting jealousy for the rest of the day, hardly able to attend to her chores or Lilo and Ellen.

"How could you do this!" she confronted Hagan the minute he stepped in the door, her gut wrenching.

"What are you talking about?" He avoided meeting her determined gaze and put his hat on the table instead of in the closet as he usually did.

"You know what I mean." She grabbed his hat off the table and flung it in the closet. "Your affair!" Her voice was laden with sarcasm. "You know how I hate deceit. How could you betray my trust?" She was shaking so hard she thought she'd fall over.

"What do you expect?" he asked in a self-righteous tone. "You're always trying to manipulate me toward what you see as right, regardless of what I might want. You're never satisfied with anything I do. I'll tell you Afra, I'm sick and tired of it." He crossed to the mantle-place and busied himself lighting his pipe.

"Hagan! How can you say that?" Hazel was right. He *had* found someone else!

"You're always criticizing me while you're allergic to criticism yourself. Are you happy with me? Are you happy with our marriage?" He walked over to her and put his hand on her shoulder.

She jumped back. "Don't you dare touch me! This isn't what all this is about! You don't really care for me after all!"

"Care for you? Care for you?" He softened somewhat. "Afra, you never let me in. You know it. When we're together there's always a part of you that holds back. On some level I don't really know you. I don't even know how you really feel about me."

She knew he was right. She had no trouble talking when her feelings weren't involved. But the minute she became emotional her stomach was in turmoil. Annoyed with herself, she said, "Hagan, I know I find it hard to let go. But that's no excuse for you to be cheating on me!" She thought she saw a glimmer of shame in his eyes, but he gave a hopeless shrug and walked out the front door.

She sank on the sofa, overcome with betrayal and the crushing feeling of abandonment.

Later, after tucking Lilo and Ellen in bed and kissing them goodnight, she went down to the parlor. Hagan was gone, but she couldn't forget his words. She knew it all, but she found it impossible to express her trapped feelings. A deep personal connection with Hagan was missing -- their love-making always faintly disappointing. Slowly they'd grown apart.

She was hurt and angry. Her head pounded. Her mind was entangled in bitter thoughts that repeated themselves over and over. She plopped down on the piano bench. Slowly she turned to the keyboard playing a note here and there. Little by little the familiar soothing music caught her up. Tchaikovsky's beautiful melodies made her soul came alive in a way she couldn't have explained.

~~

Meanwhile Hitler sat in a concert hall enraptured with one of Wagner's great mythic operas. How he identified with that glorious bygone world amidst fighting pagan gods and heroes, demons and dragons. It was a world of titanic struggle, redemption and victory. Valhalla was devoured by flames when Wotan set it on fire in a surge of self-willed annihilation.

Sitting among the exploding sounds reverberating throughout the big hall Hitler's anger, frustrations and fears faded away. His mind filled with boundless dreams of power and renown.

Chapter 4

Afra realized her marriage was a farce. She should have listened to her parents. But Hagan was amazingly handsome, an intellectual who never failed to hold her interest. She had fallen head over heels in love with him. She should have realized from the beginning he had a wandering eye. And he was right, too. Although she couldn't explain it to herself, she'd never been able to tell him how much she loved him. When they made love a part of her always held back. Regardless, she was overwhelmed with anger and jealousy. It was impossible to forgive him.

Hurriedly dressing, she ran to the kitchen and telephoned her mother, "Mutti, "I'm leaving Hagan. I'm coming home with the children."

"What can I do?" she asked her mother after they settled in. "Lilo and Ellen are unhappy and miss Hagan. I feel helpless. Mutti, I don't know what to do. I ---"

Her mother cut in. "We've all had our share of difficulties, Afra. I just thank God that we are surviving, and can still help each other. A part of your life has closed. What door will you open now?"

Afra often thought about her mother's wise words. Although weeks went by she remained consumed with bitterness. What happened to the love and passion she'd felt for Hagan? Her future looked bleak. Her father was supporting them; she couldn't get her old job back. Like everyone and everything else, the union was having financial problems and had no place for her. She wanted a home of her own and she needed part-time work to supplement the money Hagan gave her.

Two months later on Good Friday she woke up and everything seemed different. The morning sunshine streaming through the window lifted her spirits. For the first time since she left Hagan she felt free from burdensome thoughts.

She decided to go off by herself and visit Suse, who was now living in the mountains. It had been a long time since she'd seen her friend. Buoyed by this prospect, she left Ellen and Lilo in the care of her mother and boarded an early train. Slowly it wound its way up the mountainside amidst increasing forestry. At last, it stopped at a tiny station. Stepping into the morning sunshine she was caught up in a feeling that something important was about to begin.

She started off on the long walk to Suse's house in Limburg, and soon found herself in the Westervald Forest. High above, the sun illuminated the trees, generating a golden glow in the intervening fields. The sweet smell of spring filled the air.

Ahead was a small chapel with a graveyard where wildflowers grew. It was perhaps two hundred years old; the dignity of age enhanced its beauty. The simple purity of the place filled her with the peace of the Easter season. She sat down in front of a stained glass window with a picture of Jesus surrounded with glowing white light. How she yearned to walk into that picture, to be one with some long ago memory of the loving presence of Jesus Christ and His Light.

After lingering awhile, she realized it was time to be on her way. Her shoulder pack seemed weightless. Her spirits soared.

She was happier than she'd been in a long time. This pleasant mood led her to a meadow alive with the sight and sound of bees buzzing back and forth among shiny yellow flowers. Hunger struck. She sat down, reached into her shoulder pack, and pulled out a hardboiled egg and bread. When her appetite was satisfied, she lay back and rested her head on her shoulder pack.

How quiet it was, away from everything. Above her a solitary cloud hovered in the sky, an unusual cloud, shaped like an angel with wings. Slowly it descended and morphed into a real angel standing before her. Was she dreaming? She sat up.

The angel knelt beside her in the grass. He wasn't quite like the angels she'd seen at church. He was dressed in white. His wings were folded behind him. He appeared to be quite old, though he moved easily and his face was unlined. His startling blue eyes stood out in contrast to the white hair that fell about his face. He looked at her as though he knew everything and accepted it all.

"Who are you?" she asked bewildered.

Smiling, he said, "I'm your guardian angel. You can call me Pasch. It's high time we had a visit."

A faint light radiated around him. He sat on the ground and spoke of the Easter message, Christ, the crucifixion and His ascension to heaven, and what it all meant to the world. His words were eloquent, timeless.

As she listened, she began to understand. "Pasch, does this have something to do with me?"

"Yes Afra. You have a spiritual mission to help others. People will come to you. You'll be a light in the darkness. It won't be easy. There will be many sorrows. Wars will destroy large parts of the East and the West. The people will be restless and at odds with one another. But never worry. Each day will take care of itself. Your prayers will always be heard."

Afra's worries evaporated in the summer air. The sun moved from behind a cloud. Everything was brighter. She felt a weight lift from her heart.

"You must become more spiritual and dedicate your whole being to life's spiritual lessons," Pasch went on. "Then you'll be ready to fulfill your destiny. You must move to Berlin and get your own office where people will come to you for spiritual guidance."

In words she never forgot, he said:

The Spiritual Center is within you.
Climb the mountains
To the Light, to the Light!
The Sun will shine in your heart.
Climb higher and higher
Toward attunement with God's vibration.
You will never sink into evil thoughts and deeds.
And one day, in meditation, you will attain
Harmony with God's highest essence.
Your presence will help people in spiritual need.
You will see a Light shining in the night.
And its promise will be a joy to you.
Be true to yourself in your meditation
And you will have peace.
Peace that will give you wisdom.

They sat quietly. Pasch's words touched a part of her she'd never known. Although he never mentioned her desire to be a writer, a deep level of her soul opened. Enveloped in a sense of perfect peace, her sense of failure was gone. Pasch had awakened in her the idea that she could do something meaningful. With a sigh she closed her eyes and embraced that promise.

Have I been dreaming? Afra wondered when she opened her eyes and looked around. Pasch was nowhere in sight. She knew she'd better get moving. Rousing herself, she started up once more along the mountain path, her thoughts carried away by Pasch's amazing prophecies. An hour later she arrived at Suse's house.

The door flung open. "Afra! You're here! You must stay over for Easter!" Suse enthusiastically exclaimed.

"I'd love to."

In the days that followed she was silent about meeting her guardian angel, afraid Suse would think she'd imagined it in the enchanted meadow. In truth, she knew something deeply profound had happened. She needed to think it over. She spent some amiable hours with her friend until it was time to head back to Kassel.

Late in the evening when she arrived home, Lilo and Ellen were in bed. Her mother led her into the kitchen's soothing odor of freshly baked bread. There Afra felt free to share her innermost thoughts. Although she loved both of her parents, she found it easier to talk to her mother.

Mutti put the teakettle on. Afra reached up to an open shelf for the cups and set them on the table. As soon as she sat down, their yellow cat strolled in and rubbed up against her leg. "Hello Daffy." She stroked the cat's arched back. When the kettle began to whistle, Mutti lifted it off the stove to pour the water into a teapot. She put a plate of the bread on the table. Before long they were sipping tea and enjoying bread and butter.

"Mutti, I had an incredible experience in the mountains. I encountered my guardian angel!" Her voice was tinged with wonder and excitement, "His name is Pasch. He explained I have a spiritual destiny to help people and I must move to Berlin to accomplish it."

Her mother was a realistic no-nonsense woman. Yet guardian angels were a part of her religious beliefs. She believed God's angels were always nearby to guide and protect people and that they often appeared in a time of crisis. As Afra spoke about Pasch the truth of his words rang out to her in a way she couldn't ignore.

"Mutti, I can't think about anything else. Even though Pasch never said anything about writing, I would be happy to find some kind of work that would really help people."

"Afra, I've always known there was something special about you. You have a determination and will to succeed that I've rarely seen. And being dependable and caring, people will know they could always call on you and talk to you about anything." She looked at her daughter over the rim of her teacup. "Afra, go to Berlin. Your angel will take care of you, while I take care of the children."

"But I have no money."

Her mother went to the cupboard, reached in the back, and returned to the table with an old porcelain sugar jar. She took out the bit of money she'd managed to save. "Take this, Afra. Start your new life."

Chapter 5

Afra could hardly sleep she was so filled with anticipation to begin her new life. She knew there would be many possibilities in Berlin. Every day she went to church to pray for guidance. A month later she was ready to follow her destiny. She found herself surrounded by family at the station waiting for the train. Lilo clung onto her hand. They were sad to see her go.

"Look!" cried Ellen, as the train pulled up, belching steam, chugging to a halt. As usual, she was in constant motion – looking this way and that, tapping her toe, skipping around. She would have loved to come with me, thought Afra.

The conductor called, "All aboard."

Afra kissed her mother and father goodbye, gave the girls big hugs and kisses. *"Auf Wiedershen,"* they called in unison as she hurried up the steep steps of the train. She found a seat by the window and waved at her family. The train began moving down the track, gradually picking up speed. The little group passed from sight. She was alone for the first time in her life. All she had was a suitcase, and tucked away in her purse was the money Mutti had given her, just enough for one month.

She was comforted by the soft seats, clickety-clack of the wheels, and occasional sound of the engine's whistle. She closed her eyes. Her parents came into her thoughts. They'd always been supportive. She was determined to succeed in the new life about to open up for her. Right now it was like a blank screen waiting to be filled in, a hazy light in the distance, beckoning. She drifted off.

The train jerked to a stop and her eyes flew open. It seemed only minutes had passed, but they'd arrived in Berlin. People stood in the aisle reaching for luggage. For a minute she was disoriented. Did she forget anything? She picked up her suitcase and followed the other passengers into the station.

She made her way outside the building and set her suitcase on the curb. Huge buildings loomed on all sides. People hurried by, eager to get on with their day. A flock of pigeons cooed and quick stepped around on the sidewalk, their little heads making pecking movements. A car honked, and they flew up into the morning sunshine. All the activity and the bracing air filled her with a sense of excitement. She knew her experience in Berlin was going to be beyond her wildest expectations.

She had no idea of what she was going to do. Which way should she go? She could have sworn she felt a soft nudge and turned left, certain Pasch was nearby guiding her. Blocks later a bright green sign ahead caught her eye, "Room and Board: Women Only." Three freshly scrubbed steps led to the front door. Inside the hallway was a door with a sign, "Manager." She rang the bell. The door was opened by a motherly looking woman with graying hair pulled back in a bun. *"Guten morgan,"* she said.

"Guten morgan. I am Frau Waesch. I've just arrived in Berlin and need a room."

"Welcome Frau Waesch. I'm Frau Weber," she smoothed her hands over her head, though not a hair was out of place. "I have a nice room for you," she said and led Afra upstairs. The room was simply furnished but was bright and airy with a window overlooking the back yard. A slightly worn quilt on the bed gave it a homey look, and it was priced within her modest budget. She knew she'd be comfortable.

The next morning she arose early. She was in a buoyant mood, ready to explore the city and determine exactly what she was there for.

This was spacious Berlin -- with parks and little canals everywhere -- lots of trees and violet lilacs -- people sitting on benches -- pigeons strutting around looking for handouts.

She walked along the stately tree-lined boulevard Unter den Linden, taking in the handsome Crown Prince Palace, St. Hedwig's Cathedral, the meandering River Spree. At the western end was the towering Brandenburg Gate, topped with a statue of the goddess of peace riding in a chariot drawn by four horses.

She strolled down Kurfurstendamm, an elegant street with fine hotels, fashionable shops, big restaurants and cabarets. Sidewalk cafes were crowded with high-spirited Berliners gearing up for another day.

She walked through squares filled with statues of forgotten heroes, streets named after national heroes. She stood in the shadows of monumental government buildings. The Reichstag, Germany's legislature, was fronted with six Corinthian pillars. The great doors were kept locked, giving the impression that something very serious and important must be going on inside. Berlin seemed to epitomize a German respect for solidity and history.

Unexpectedly a passerby grasped her arm and pulled her into the entrance of a building. "What are you doing?" Afra cried out in panic.

Shh, shh, Fraulein," whispered the man. "Don't you see those Nazis marching down the street carrying their flag with the swastika? If you stay out on the sidewalk and fail to raise your arm to greet the flag, they will beat you up."

Afra cautiously stuck her head out. Other pedestrians had also ducked into doorways. "That's awful!" she exclaimed in a nervous whisper. "They beat up women too?"

"Well, even if they only shoved you around or roughed you up, it wouldn't be a pleasant experience, would it? Please don't get upset, Fraulein," he consoled her. "Berlin is full of this kind of thing these days. You'll get used to it."

"I'd never get used to brutality! But thank you for helping me." The marchers passed, their jackboots pounding the pavement. Afra and the stranger said goodbye and went their separate ways.

She walked all over Berlin for a day and a half with still no idea of why she was there. "Pasch," she silently called, "my feet hurt and I'm tired. Please help me find my way."

In an instant she knew she should go back to the boarding house. To her relief, the door to her landlady's apartment was open. The radio was playing. She knocked. Frau Weber came to the door in a flowered dressing gown and slippers.

"Well, hello Frau Waesch. Won't you come in?" She turned off the radio. "Would you like a cup of coffee and a slice of honey cake?" She gestured toward the kitchen.

"That would be nice." Frau Weber led her to the kitchen. The smell of sausages, sauerkraut and fried onions drifted through the window from a nearby building reminding Afra it was time for lunch.

"Please make your self at home," said Frau Weber.

"Thank you," Afra replied as she sat, grateful to slip off her shoes under the table. Her landlady was so warm and friendly; she felt she could trust her, that she would understand her situation. "I was hoping you might be able to give me some advice." While they sipped coffee and ate cake she told her about Pasch, how he had revealed her destiny on the mountain, and her search for what she needed to do in Berlin.

Frau Weber had an idea. "I know a palm reader, Herr Reyes, a very spiritual man. I think he can tell you."

Afra couldn't think of anything else to do, so she made an appointment with him for the following day. But when he greeted her at the door she saw that, although he was a gypsy, he was also an ordinary looking man of slender build with deep-set eyes, thinning hair. They introduced themselves, and Herr Reyes directed her to a small, round table.

"Can you tell me why I'm here in Berlin and what I must do?" she asked.

"Certainly, Frau Waesch." He took her hands, closely examined her palms. "You have strong psychic ability. You should be doing this instead of me."

Afra was speechless. Had she come all the way to Berlin just to be a gypsy palm reader? What would her mother think? Even worse, her father would be aghast.

Herr Reyes was still focused on her palms. "You must channel your psychic gift," he said, pointing to a deep line on her palm. "You must study astrology to learn how to help people." He looked up. "I know an astrologer who can help you. Her name is Frau Brecht. Wait a minute. I'll give her a call."

Afra reached for her purse. She had to get out of there. But already he was giving the number to the operator. Didn't he know that only eccentrics went to astrologers? For the life of her, she couldn't imagine studying astrology, much less making a living at it.

Before she could interrupt, he was talking to Frau Brecht. He told her briefly about Afra and handed her the phone.

"Hello, Frau Waesch," she said. "Herr Reyes speaks highly of you. Do you happen to type, my dear?"

Afra described her background.

"Oh, you do type!" exclaimed Frau Brecht. "Good. I can pay you to help me. I am writing a book on astrology."

Afra was dumbfounded. Would she become, of all things, a writer of astrology books? Perhaps there was something here for her to learn.

The money wasn't all that much, but Afra remembered Pasch's strong urging that she go to Berlin to follow a spiritual destiny. She worked eight-hour days. Her new employer was a thorough professional. When she worked, her books, charts and graphs were scattered on the table. More books were piled on the floor nearby. Afra's first reaction was that she could never work in that way – to glean so much information from so many sources and make a prognosis. Still, it was a valuable lesson if, perhaps in the future, she might be involved in similar work. For the moment she was too much of a beginner to even think of learning astrology this way. After a month she quit.

The time wasn't wasted. Afra had discovered that Frau Brecht had a large clientele of respectable people and that she did very well financially. Frau Brecht told her about a school of astrology. Its teachers were Vehlow and Froehling, two astrologers famous in Germany with well-known books on the subject.

Afra had an unshakable belief that her life was now under the direction of some higher order. She went with it.

Chapter 6

She sat in one of Berlin's open-air cafes and ordered a Deutches beefsteak burger, home-fried potatoes and cucumber salad. She leaned back in her chair with a sigh of satisfaction. She had found a better paying job and was on her way to enroll at Herr Froehling's Astrology Academy.

A few blocks further on she spotted the academy in a Freemason's lodge. It took her a minute or two to find the inconspicuous entrance on the side of the building. The reception area was no more than a dimly lit hallway with a table displaying an assortment of astrology books and a chipper old lady seated at a well-worn desk.

"Can I help you, Fraulein?" she asked as Afra approached her.

"Thank you. Have you an astrology course I can take?"

"Of course. Are you a beginning student?"

"Yes, I am."

A few brief answers satisfied the receptionist that she was sincere. "Now, do you want to study with Herr Froehling or Herr Vehlow?"

"Both!" Afra answered at once.

She did indeed study with both distinguished gentlemen, but most of her classes were with Herr Froehling.

On her first day she entered the classroom for beginning students. It was a big room with a high ceiling, tall windows. Like a stage, the area in front was raised about eight inches. Two big blackboards faced the class. A wooden podium stood off to one side.

She found a place at one of the schoolroom desks. Soon about twenty-five students were ready and waiting for the class to begin. She had no idea so many people were interested in astrology, but during that time of economic and political uncertainty people were looking for something to brighten their often penny pinching, dreary lives.

She had always lumped astrologers and fortunetellers together, imagined them in turbans and colorful clothes, festooned with jewelry. Yet, like Afra, her classmates were average looking, conservatively dressed in the usual brown, gray and beige. Seated on one side of her was a man with a big nose and cropped hair. On the other side was a prim looking woman with glasses, hair neatly in a bun, dressed in a blouse and black skirt.

Afra sensed radiant vitality and curious electricity in the atmosphere. It had to be Herr Froehling entering the room, striding down the aisle. Big, with broad shoulders, a strong face and an abundance of reddish hair, he caught her curious stare. She quickly turned away.

Ignoring the step to the platform, he nonchalantly jumped up and walked to the podium where he sorted out his notes. Afra noticed his bright yellow tie, a contrast to his brownish tweed jacket. Like a man at home in the spotlight, one way or another, he stood out in a crowd.

He held everyone's attention. "My name is Herr Froehling," he said in a sonorous voice. "And I welcome every one of you."

His eyes swept over the class. His hands on the podium, he was an image of strength and authority. "Your horoscope is a map of the heavens drawn up for your date, time and place of birth. The planetary vibrations at that moment affect you for the rest of your life. Your horoscope shows your talents and abilities, as well as weaknesses in your character. Of course, some of us have easier planetary patterns than others, but there is nothing static in the universe. You can change yourself by changing your thoughts, your attitudes, and the way you respond to people and situations. However, everything is a struggle for those who hold onto ego and self-will."

Standing with focused attention, he explained, "There are twelve Sun Signs. The dates of each Sun Sign may vary a little from year to year. Aries, the first sign of the Zodiac, falls approximately between March 21 and April 21."

Afra knew she was an Aries, born April 10.

Herr Froehling picked up a piece of chalk and with a flourish drew a symbol on the blackboard, ♈. "This symbol depicts Aries. It represents the horned Ram that dashes head first toward its goal. However, Arian impulsiveness and inability to listen to advice can get them in trouble."

Afra's mind flashed on that tumultuous time when she was bent on marrying Hagan despite her parents' warnings.

Herr Froehling explained, "It's important for Arians to surrender self-will to the will of God. Then God's light and power shines through them to illumine dark places, bringing hope and courage to others."

He glanced at his copious notes. "Each sign rules a different part of the body. Aries rules the head, denoting a quick mind, a great desire for knowledge."

Oh yes! Afra thought, high-spirited now that she was pursuing astrology, a subject she already found fascinating.

Herr Froehling continued, "The Sun Signs are divided into the four elements: Fire, Earth, Air and Water. Aries is a fire sign, represented by a red-hot flame that flares up then dies out quickly. It's the untamed fire of impulse and ardor."

Afra's cheeks grew hot. That's what had happened with Hagan. All the passion she felt for him died. She never really knew him. She didn't even understand her own needs.

Froehling then described the rest of the Sun Signs and asked the students to study them in detail. He drew a circle with a dot in the middle and the figure of a crescent Moon.

$$\odot \qquad \mathbb{D}$$

He said, "The dot within the circle is the symbol for the Sun. The Sun in your horoscope depicts your basic character, your individuality that is expressed through the sign in which it's placed. For example, the Aries person's individuality is expressed through the sign Aries."

He drew the symbol for Aries beside the Sun.

$$\odot \quad \aries$$

"In this case, we say their sun sign is in Aries. Basically, like the Ram, Arians are daring self–starters, always moving ahead."

I can certainly relate to that, thought Afra.

"The Moon and the sign it resides in describe your subconscious and your emotions. Although the Sun and Moon are luminaries, we consider them as planets for convenience sake." He turned again to the blackboard and drew the symbols for the planets.

$$\mercury \qquad \venus \qquad \mars \qquad \jupiter \qquad \saturn \qquad \uranus \qquad \neptune$$

Mercury Venus Mars Jupiter Saturn Uranus Neptune
(Note: Pluto at that time had not yet been discovered.)

"These planets have additional characteristics that influence your life." He tapped the symbol for Mercury with the chalk. "Mercury represents your conscious, reasoning mind, and the way you communicate."

"Venus is the planet of love, peace and harmony. It's also related to beauty, artistry and music."

"Look at the shape of this planet," said Froehling as he pointed a sharp finger at Mars. "Mars is an outgoing, out-thrusting energy. At its best, it gives courage and a drive to accomplish, to progress. At its worst it's destructive, angry and cruel."

Herr Froehling bounded off the platform and strode down the aisle as he spoke. "Each country is under a planet. Germany is ruled by Mars, the opposite of feminine, peaceful and loving Venus. Mars is the planet of war, and Germany has always had a militaristic tradition. Many of our young men prefer the discipline, challenges and excitement of military life to the dull placidity of peace. But even in peacetime there is a love here of military music, marching parades, uniforms, flag waving and organized groups with a militant cast." He leapt back onto the platform.

Like an actor changing the mood in a play, a benign smile filled his face and he spoke in mellow tones. "Jupiter is the lucky planet that encourages optimism, expansiveness and good judgment."

"Herr Froehling," asked a man with a round, jovial face, "is there a negative side to Jupiter? In my horoscope Mercury squares Jupiter."

"A good point, Willi. All the planets have both a positive and negative side. We respond to them depending on how they are placed and their aspects in our charts. When two planets 'square' each other they are approximately 90 degrees apart, denoting a conflict between the planets. When Mercury, the mental planet, squares Jupiter, there's a tendency to poor judgment and imprudence -- to speak without thought of the consequences."

Herr Froehling looked directly at Willi to be sure he understood. "Therefore, Willi, make it a habit to think carefully before you speak and avoid getting carried away with wild opinions and extravagant claims."

Willi laughed at himself and everyone joined in. "You're so right, Herr Froehling. My big mouth is always getting me into trouble. I speak too freely."

Froehling nodded and turned his attention to the next planet. "Saturn confers duty, dependability and patience. At its highest, it's loyal, serious, hard working and ambitious."

Afra could easily relate to Saturn. She was ambitious, a hard worker.

"If negative," Herr Froehling added, "Saturn is a callous user and harsh disciplinarian. There's also a Saturnian influence here in Germany: obsession with bureaucracy, strict discipline, attention to duty, unwavering obedience to authority, and the need always to make a proper impression.

This reminded Afra of an incident when she was pregnant. She was washing the supper dishes sitting in front of the sink instead of standing, because her back hurt.

"Afra!" her mother exclaimed. "How can you do such a thing? You know the neighbors can see into the kitchen. What in the world will they think?"

Herr Froehling interrupted her thoughts. "Still with us, Frau Waesch?" Before she could blink, he said to the class, "Uranus rules astrology and the occult. In a birth chart, it represents originality, freedom and unpredictable events. On the negative side, it's erratic, rebellious and unconventional.

"Neptune represents your intuitive or psychic capacity and relates to the mysterious and hidden side of life."

Afra wondered about Neptune in her horoscope, her intuitive hunches often proved correct.

"In conclusion," said Herr Froehling as he walked behind the podium, "I suggest you memorize the planets, signs, keywords and approximate dates for the Sun Signs. Your memory over time will become an easily accessible data bank."

Afra threw herself into her studies. After the tedious years she had spent at trade school and the labor union, she knew the comprehensive science of astrology would always hold her interest. It was fascinating to dig down, to fully understand herself and others. She was determined to become a professional astrologer. She had just enough money to have Herr Froehling draw up a horoscope wheel for her date, time and place of birth. It revealed her Sun and Mercury sextiled Neptune.

~~

While Afra was immersing herself in the study of astrology, Hitler was being schooled by his mentor Dietrich Eckart. A hard-drinking journalist, poet and playwright, Eckart was a member of a large circle of occultists called The Thule Group. He taught Hitler how to use the Three Powers of Manifestation: visualization, single-minded intention, and strength of will. More significantly, Eckart was the Master Adept of a secret inner core of satanists within the Thulists. He initiated Hitler in a ghastly ritual of Black Magic to give him extraordinary supernatural ability.

In the middle of Eckart's rite there appeared before Hitler a tall imposing apparition with piercing, coal-black eyes and raven hair. It was the Dark Spirit – once more evoked by Hitler's evil mindset and moral nature.

I can use this man, thought the demon. "Do as I instruct you," he commanded, "and you will accrue power and fame beyond your wildest dreams."

Unfortunately, Hitler had no idea of what he was getting himself into. But he was becoming aware the visible universe had an invisible counterpart. The lower planes were dark and foreboding, inhabited by evil spirits that served only those who corrupt and destroy.

The higher planes were occupied by good and beautiful spirits, such as Afra's guardian angel. While Afra was blessed with Pasch to protect her and to develop her spiritual wisdom, Hitler became the demon's tool.

Chapter 7

Afra walked briskly down the street to the Astrology Academy with planetary information and mathematical formulas racing through her mind. Already she was gaining deeper insights. She knew that once she had a thorough knowledge of the age-old science, she'd transform her life and the lives of many clients. Her determination increased.

Arriving at the academy, she found a seat near the front. Repeatedly a distinguished looking man with gray-flecked hair removed himself to a seat further down the aisle whenever she sat near him. But she had more important things to think about.

Herr Froehling's method was to put up the horoscope of a famous person or someone in the public eye, perhaps President von Hindenburg, Benito Mussolini or Andres Segovia. She wondered whose horoscope Herr Froehling would be using to teach delineation that evening. There he was -- drawing Adolph Hitler's chart on the blackboard. As Afra copied the symbols for the planets she had a foreboding of potential malevolence.

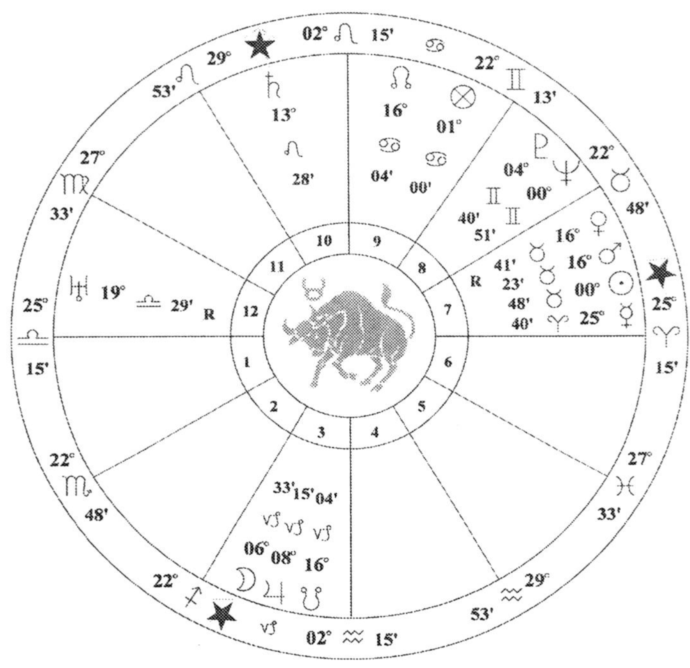

At the podium Froehling, with his usual cheerful welcome, began his delineation. "Hitler is a native of Taurus, the sign that falls between April 21 and May 21." He pointed to the symbols for the Sun and Taurus. ☉ ♉ "Now class, keep in mind that while each sign has certain basic characteristics, they can differ widely. Taurus is ruled by Venus, a sociable planet." A small smile crossed Herr Froehling's face. "I've heard that Hitler can be most charming."

Froehling held up five fingers. "He has five planets in earth signs: the Sun, Venus and Mars in Taurus and the Moon and Jupiter in Capricorn. What is the main characteristic for those with a preponderance of earth signs?" Froehling scanned the room, certain of an answer to his simple question.

The man Afra had noticed earlier spoke up, "They are materialistic; and Taureans, in particular, love ownership. If the individual is a negative type, he's overly possessive and greedy. His fears make him think he never has enough."

"You are right, Herr Beyer," said Froehling. Security on all levels is the fundamental principle of Hitler's life." He turned back to the class. "The signs are also divided into quadruplicities: cardinal, fixed and mutable. Taurus, Leo, Scorpio and Aquarius are fixed signs. When fixed signs predominate in a horoscope the individual has fixity of purpose and is unswervingly stubborn.

Hitler has the Sun, Venus and Mars in Taurus and Saturn in Leo. When he makes up his mind, he refuses to change it." Froehling walked behind the podium and leaned forward on his elbows. "Although Taureans often have a lazy side, once they have a definite goal, they will stay with it long after everyone else has given up."

He pointed to Venus on the blackboard. "With the Sun, Venus and Mars in earthy Taurus: sex, money and possessions are extremely important to Hitler. Although he has five planets in earth signs, there are no planets in water. Do you remember the qualities of the water signs?"

Afra raised her hand. She had four planets in water and felt she understood their qualities. "When water is emphasized in a chart, it quickens the emotions, feelings and sympathies."

"Thank you, Frau Waesch. With no planets in water, Hitler is devoid of feeling, only concerned about people as a means to an end. With the emphasis on earth signs, he tries to compensate for his lack of feeling through controlling others and the acquisition of money, possessions and land."

Froehling arranged his notes in order and announced, "Let's take a ten minute break."

Afra went into the hall with the others. It was good to stretch her legs. A few people were at the counter browsing or buying astrology books. Others gathered in groups involved in animated conversations. Ten minutes later they were all back in their seats.

Froehling had put up a wheel showing the twelve houses. "As you know by now, each house is a sector assigned to a different department of life. The Sun, Venus and Mars in the 7th House show that Hitler's life is entangled with other people. Only in problem-laden atmosphere of conflicting ambitions, plans and desires does he truly feel at home.

Herr Froehling gripped the sides of the podium, holding the class in a steady gaze. "Square aspects involve two or more planets that are 90 degrees apart. They indicate obstacles and challenges. Squares in fixed signs indicate destructive patterns over many lifetimes and refusal to change. With Mars and Venus making fixed squares to Saturn, Hitler is driven to force people to bend to his will and to manipulate conditions to comply with his own immovable opinions." Froehling's voice raised a notch. "When thwarted, he explodes in a rage."

Afra wondered if Herr Froehling was a Leo, with his sense of the dramatic. He seemed to get right into the role of the character he was describing.

"Ordinarily Saturn in the 10th House denotes hard work, discipline, responsibility and organization that bring professional success and positions of authority. However, Saturn squared by Mars and Venus signify that Hitler alternates between laziness and ruthless aggression. He has no scruples against having his army of roughnecks use terrorist methods to subdue political opposition."

Froehling paced back and forth across the stage. "He is unable to love himself, so he longs for absolute loyalty and wild displays of admiration from his followers. But nothing will ever stave his desperate hunger for more."

Froehling stopped his pacing and spoke with conviction. "Real love makes no demands on anyone. The power isn't in being loved; the power is in giving love. Loving others is its own reward."

Afra noted down Froehling's statements, and then looked up quickly. She didn't want to miss anything.

"At the same time, things are seldom black or white. The five favorable 120 degree trine aspects involving Hitler's Taurus planets and the Moon and Jupiter in Capricorn denote an uncanny ability to convince others. Already he has a good deal of leadership in the Nazi Party. He does have concern for the welfare of the public. However, as shown by the overriding squares, he is deathly afraid of losing control. Ultimately, tyranny and abuse of power will result in disgrace and downfall."

Chapter 8

He's doing it again! Afra thought with irritation. As she was leaving Herr Froehling's class the man called Herr Beyer edged away from her. Though too proud to show it, she was hurt. Why should I care about some guy I don't even know? Afra mused. But she felt she had to confront him. If she didn't, she knew she'd become increasingly resentful. Reluctantly she walked over to him. "Pardon me, Herr Beyer," she looked him straight in the eye. "May I ask why you always distance yourself from me?"

"Frau Waesch," he answered, stepping back, "since you asked I'll answer you truthfully. As a long time student of metaphysics, I'm able to read auras." He noted her confusion and explained. "Auras are energy fields that emanate from people and reflect their inner being. Clairvoyants see the aura of a loving and harmonious person as lightness and radiance." He softened his tone, knowing it's not always easy to accept the truth. "Frau Waesch, your aura is filled with an anger that literally pushes me away."

She looked at him stunned. That couldn't be. Was he some nut? Was she such an awful person? She still harbored a lot of anger against Hagan. Was it that bad? She looked more closely at Herr Beyer. He had a scholar's face – intelligent, with a broad brow and thoughtful eyes.

"Perhaps," he ventured, "we could go for coffee at the cafe down the street, and you could tell me what seems to be troubling you."

She could tell by his kind expression that he was truly concerned. So after they found a quiet table in the cafe she told him about her angry separation from her husband and how she'd left her children with her parents, inwardly compelled to come to Berlin.

He revealed he was a Studienrat, an upper-level schoolteacher and had been working with astrology for fifteen years. "I still find Herr Froehling's classes interesting," he said. "I enjoy coming here now and then."

Afra put forth the question burning inside her. "Herr Beyer, is there anything I can do to fix my aura?"

"Of course. The way is simple, but carrying it out won't be easy. You see, auras are electromagnetic fields radiating from us. They are made up of colors ranging from dark and murky to clear and radiant. These colors are affected by thoughts and emotions. Think of the pictures of Jesus with the beautiful golden aura surrounding his head. To regain the beauty of your aura, you must forgive your ex-husband. Can you do this?"

"I guess I'm going to have to," she said, resigned. At that moment she felt every unpleasant incident from her marriage still embedded in her memory. It was time to leave that behind her, clean up her aura and get on with her life.

In the months that followed she forgave Hagan again and again when bad feelings returned.

As time went on she began to know Egon better. As the months passed, he seemed more comfortable in her presence. He seemed even to like her a little. Hopefully, her aura was clearing.

One evening when Herr Froehling's lecture was over, Egon beckoned to her. Standing next to him was the young man who'd spoken up in her first class. "Afra, I'd like you to meet Willi." Willi's eyes twinkled with good humor. A big smile crossed his face as they shook hands. "Willi has been doing a lot of research on Hitler. I think he'll write a book about him."

Ah, thought Afra. That could get him into serious trouble.

Egon interrupted her thoughts. "We're going for coffee at the café. Would you like to join us?"

"Thank you, I'd enjoy that," she answered, anticipating an interesting discussion of astrology.

Willi swung open the door of the café to the sounds of animated conversation, the scrape of chairs, flatware on china in an atmosphere of cigarette smoke, hot coffee, and sausage on the grill. Egon and Afra studied the menu. Willi pulled a ceramic ashtray to him, shook a cigarette from a crumpled packet and lit up. "Have you tried the streuselkuchen, Afra? I heartily recommend it."

"That sounds fine to me."

One of the waitresses strolled over.

"Three streuselkuchen and coffee, please," said Willi. He was wearing a shaggy sweater and looked like a man totally relaxed and comfortable with himself.

"Are you really thinking of writing a book about Hitler?" asked Afra.

"Yes, I am. Adolph Hitler is not just another figure in our current political arena. Egon and I are convinced whether we like it or not, he's going to be a powerful leader in our country."

"Based on his horoscope?"

"Of course," Willi tapped his cigarette on the ashtray. "Astrology tells everything that lies beneath the surface. For example, Hitler has two fixed stars in his horoscope."

"What's a fixed star?" she asked. Every time she thought she was beginning to understand astrology there was something more to pique her interest.

"A fixed star," said Willi, "contrasts with what the ancients called wandering stars that we know as planets. Often a fixed star in conjunction with a planet sets famous and infamous people apart from the common man. Hitler's Saturn close to the fixed star Acubens denotes strong leadership, showmanship, and a faculty for understanding the needs of people weaker than he is. He envisions a grand destiny for Germany, sweeping people away with compelling oration and suggestive intoxication."

Afra was eager to hear more of Willi's insights. "I can see that fixed stars are another fascinating part of astrology."

Willi elaborated, "I must tell you Afra. Acubens has a malevolent side brought out by Saturn's destructive squares with Venus and Mars in Hitler's horoscope. These factors portend a ruthless rise to power followed by a disastrous ending."

The waitress set the streuselkuchen and steaming cups of coffee on the table.

When she left, Egon said, "Actually, Hitler's entire persona is affected by those squares. But Venus, the love planet, is retrograde as depicted by the little Rx by it, indicating a kind of introversion and holding back. And with Venus and Mars squaring Saturn, we can conclude Hitler is partially or totally impotent." Egon paused and stirred his coffee. "Yet there's a preoccupation with sex and great turmoil within due to his frustrated sex drive. Thus, when he's finally able to express the submerged part of his personality it would be compulsive and abnormal."

Afra gave a self-conscious laugh.

Willi smiled at her naiveté. He shook the last cigarette out of the pack. "The Moon conjuncts the fixed star Facies, also suggesting sexual impotency or perversion. Hitler's thoughts and instincts about sex are masochistic, wanting someone to debase or inflict pain on him."

Afra was shocked. She knew that sexual energy was the strongest drive in the world, but had no idea it could be so distorted.

"Hitler holds his audiences spellbound," Willi resumed as he blew out a long stream of smoke that hung in the air. "The men are convinced he's Germany's savior and adoring women besiege him. They haven't an inkling that his oratorical skills are only an outlet for his repressed sexual force. That isn't real potency."

Almost reluctantly, they began eating.

Egon asked Willi, "Didn't you tell me you once met Hitler's half-brother at one of the beer hall talks?"

"That's right. He told me their father used to beat Adolph unmercifully with a rhinoceros hide dog whip. On one occasion he choked him until he lost consciousness."

"How awful!" Egon exclaimed. "When a Taurus child is denied love or badly treated, he'll try to find fulfillment through power and control rather than love."

Willi added, "Just take another look at Facies. It's said that where cruelty, violence, suicide and murder are involved, Facies is likely to be involved. In my opinion Hitler has an ice-cold heart."

Egon added, "When Venus is retrograde the inhibited love nature often finds an outlet through art or music. Hitler is known to be a fervent lover of Wagner's music. I'd venture to say that for him Wagner's operas of Germany's great historical victories and heroic warriors inspire him with a power he absorbs into himself."

Afra was stunned by Egon's words. To her chagrin both she and Hitler had Venus retrograde in Taurus, and they both had a common love of music. However, she was particularly fond of Tchaikovsky's sweet melodies.

Egon's voice roused her from her ponderings. "As a young man Hitler dreamed of being a great artist. However, his pictures were lifeless and he was incapable of any kind of disciplined or systematic work. Twice he was turned down by the Vienna Academy of Art. Following those devastating failures, he put in short hours painting post cards or writing. He spent most of his time wandering through streets and parks, staring at buildings he admired, or visiting the library. There he read the political news of the day and books on history, occultism, magic, hypnotism and astrology."

Afra lifted her hands in disbelief. "Are you saying Hitler is an astrologer?"

Egon looked thoughtful, "It's my guess that although he may think he knows a lot about astrology, he probably just dabbles at it."

Chapter 9

After speaking to Egon for a few minutes on the phone, Afra plunged into the purpose of her call. She was beginning to understand there was far more to astrology than reading character and predicting the future. How she longed to inspire and reform people to live on a higher spiritual plane. She knew there was much Egon could teach her about this side of astrology. "Egon, I was wondering if you ever take private students."

"You will make a fine astrologer, Afra. I'd be happy to take you on as a student." They agreed on a price before hanging up.

In her first lesson Egon explained: "In many ways astrology could be called a science of symbols that suggest universal truths of the heavens. By learning to let go of your conscious mind and negative emotions, you'll discover the symbols will help you comprehend a higher spiritual law."

"Egon, since I began to know you I've come to realize, more than anything, I want to be a spiritual astrologer."

His smile told her he was pleased. "Troublesome times give us the impetus to correct past mistakes, reconnect with our Higher Selves and create other possibilities. Let me show you."

He picked up her horoscope from the other charts on the table.

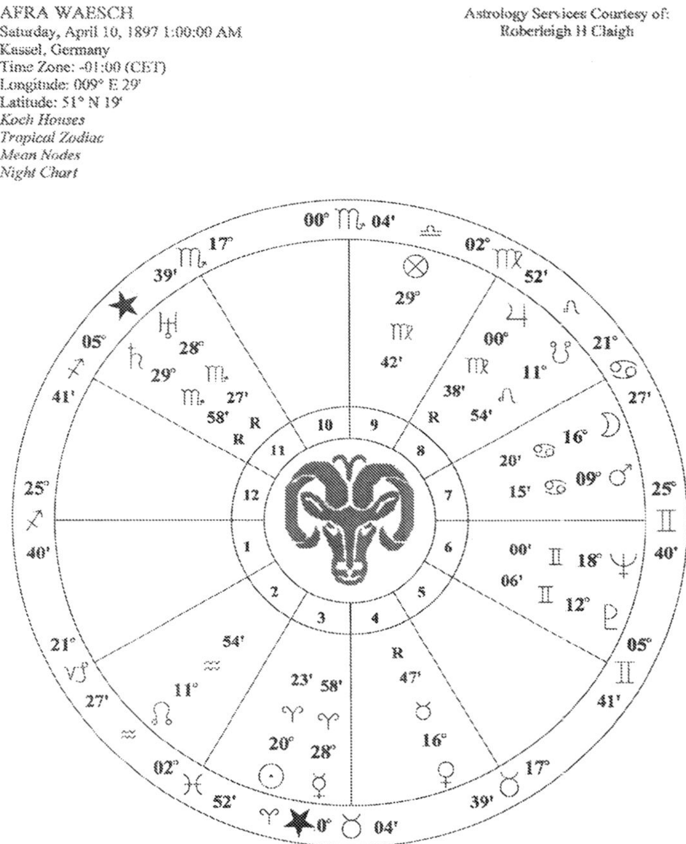

"To quickly review the basics, the Sun and Mercury in Aries show you have initiative and energy and like to be in charge. You're intelligent with a quick and very active mind. He then pointed to the planets and Ascendant that formed a Grand Trine in her horoscope (☉ ☿ △ ♃ △ Asc.). This fortunate Grand Trine shows good karma." Afra listened intently.

"The trine aspects to Jupiter indicate you have strong inner faith brought in from past lifetimes. You want to reach out and find God, for Jupiter is the planet of religion. With Jupiter, in the 8th House you tune into the astral planes. Also, Jupiter in this house is a guardian angel who guides you through adversity and brings you blessings."

Egon's appraisal was such a comfort she felt she could tell him about Pasch. "Egon, what you say is true. I do have a guardian angel. His name is Pasch and he comes to me in person or like a silent knowing when I need him. He's the reason I'm studying astrology here in Berlin."

"I'm not surprised. You wouldn't be studying astrology if you weren't interested in helping people. And you certainly wouldn't be interested in spiritual astrology."

"But Egon, it's so hard for me to express my emotions. It's like I'm locked inside of myself," embarrassed, she dropped her eyes.

"I know," he said gently. "With Venus retrograde at the time of your birth, it's difficult for you to express love openly regardless of how deeply you feel."

"Egon, Hitler also has Venus retrograde. Not only that, we both have Venus in Taurus!" It was painful for to think of a similarity between her chart and that terrible man.

"Yes, that's so. Although Hitler can be extraordinarily charming and cordial, on a deep level it's impossible for him to let go. Don't forget that Hitler's Venus and Mars square Saturn in Leo so he's coldhearted and vengeful. But Afra, in your horoscope, Venus sextiles the Moon and Mars. In spite of feeling restrained you have a loving nature and sincerely like people. You show your affection by helping others."

He's right, thought Afra.

"In addition, your Venus is placed in the 4th House that represents your home and the roots of your being. Your innermost self is filled with love. Though hidden, people sense it and are drawn to you. But first you must be sure that you've overcome every last remnant of bitterness and anger."

Afra nodded in agreement. She asked, "Would you please give me your analysis of my Saturn/Uranus conjunction?"

"Of course. These two closely conjoined planets in Scorpio play a potent role because they are by themselves in half of the wheel. They denote psychic ability that enables you to pick up on all kinds of things other people are unaware of." He looked at her closely. "Shall I go on?"

"Yes, Egon," she urged, her face a study in concentration.

"Saturn in Scorpio is reserved with moods of withdrawal. It's why you don't have an extroverted personality so typical of your Aries Sun Sign and Sagittarius Ascendant.

"Although your life is not an easy one, you're an old soul whose mission appears to be inspiring and teaching others." He raised a finger to make a final point. "Every one of us is on the way to the mountaintop of spiritual consciousness." He dropped his hand. "There are many paths and sooner or later we all arrive at the same place."

Chapter 10

Afra and Egon walked to one of Hitler's jam-packed Nazi meetings. Despite Herr Froehling's interpretation of his badly afflicted horoscope, she was curious to hear the man who was fast becoming a prominent figure in Berlin.

"Hitler is a dynamic speaker," Egon told her, "and has a remarkable talent for drawing new members to the Nazi Party."

Afra said, "I remember when it was just a small group of men called the German Workers' Party."

"You can't imagine how different that party is now. No sooner did Hitler become a member than he somehow contrived to gain control. Ultimately, he was elected to first chairman with dictatorial powers."

"Are you serious? Dictatorial powers? That sounds ominous."

Egon nodded in agreement.

They approached a huge building and joined the crowd pressing to get in. They found two seats and watched as 10,000 Berliners filled the hall. The people were drawn to Hitler's charismatic speech making and the National Socialists positive appeals – family, community, homeland, and a desire to have things better.

While the band played a stirring overture, a nervous Hitler and his deputy, Rudolph Hess, waited in the lobby. When Hitler first started speaking for the German Socialist Party he had often faced opposition and sometimes contempt.

But then his mind turned to Karl Haushofer, a brilliant professor of Political Geography whom he greatly admired. Haushofer's goal was to help Germans think in terms of whole continents. It was a strong ideology for a defeated nation that had been forced to hand over part of its home territory and all of its colonies to the victors. In his opinion geo-politics was justification for world conquest. Hitler remembered his words, "Think in terms of great spaces, of whole continents and oceans, and thereby direct your course."

Fueled by those thoughts, Hitler had absolute confidence his speech would imbue every last person there with the desire to regain status as a nation to be reckoned with.

The music ended. Hess walked to the stage and stood in front of an oversized party banner. He was a square jawed man with slightly buck-teeth and thick eyebrows overshadowing deep-set eyes. They were clear blue, but with a disconcerting somnambulistic quality. Afra wondered why Hitler had chosen him to speak; he seemed to be uncomfortable before the large audience. After he announced Hitler, storm troopers marched in. They stood at attention along the wide center aisle. With perfect timing a spotlight played on Hitler as he slowly strode past them. Thunderous cries of "Heil! Heil!" filled the hall as row after row of people raised their arms in stiff salutes.

Hitler mounted the stage and faced his audience. The audience fell silent, waiting for the highlight of the evening. Afra scrutinized him closely. It was the first time she'd seen him in person. She recognized the toothbrush moustache, dark hair plastered at an angle across his forehead, hands clasped together in front of his crotch. While his face was coarse and undistinguished, his unusual eyes drew her attention. They were a strange, almost fluorescent blue.

He began speaking, hesitant, gradually feeling his way. Then suddenly a rush of adrenaline streamed through his body as his powerful Fuhrer persona emerged. His voice rang out in a tone of absolute authority that captured everyone in its spell. Intuitively tapping into the secret sufferings and humiliations of his audience, he expelled their frustrations on targets he placed before them. He exploited their desires for national aggrandizement. He criticized the Weimar Republican for conforming to the gigantic reparations the victors exacted after Germany lost the war. "It's inconceivable that we could ever pay the unrealistic sum of $65 billion dollars!" he fumed. "To say nothing of the fact that we were never the sole cause of the war!"

His audience gave a shout of approval. Afra found herself caught up in a collective wave of emotion and memory -- her father away fighting for four long years, how they'd been stripped of national pride after their defeat, the sacrifices they'd endured.

Hitler spoke with fervor, "Although our enemies left us shackled with no hope for the future, I will heal the wounds of that treacherous war and make the Fatherland great! Under my leadership, Germany will regain its power and become even greater and stronger than it once was!" He flung his arms up and smashed his fist against the palm of his other hand. He held everyone under a hypnotic spell by the sheer force of his conviction. The mesmerized crowd believed every promise.

It appeared to Egon that there was something about Hitler's eyes that reminded him of a medium in a trance. During his moments of great intensity, it appeared as if another being spoke out of his body – as if he was possessed by supernatural powers.

Suddenly Hitler shouted in strident tones, "We are not only surrounded by enemies outside of Germany, but inside as well! Ever since the war we've been inundated by Polish and Russian Jews." His histrionics created a frenzied atmosphere. "Those Jews have taken advantage of our country's impoverished condition.

How did they do this? By greedily buying up our businesses and real estate!"

A growl arose from the audience. They deeply resented the Jews for their wealth.

Hitler shouted about his strength and determination. "I stand on the principle that what I feel about my country is not only worthy of recognition, it must be followed to the end. I am your leader and that must be the beginning and end of your political faith!" His voice rose to a passionate climax. "My will is the will of Germany -- the will of every Aryan in the Reich. Not two wills but one – MINE!!"

The audience rose in a rush and gave him thunderous unending applause. In Hitler they found their leader, the embodiment of their cause.

Afra listened to the din that filled the immense hall. It was clear how finely attuned Hitler was to the people. As she and Egon walked home, Hitler's fanatic words reverberated in her head. "My will is the will of Germany." How dreadful! Not at all in keeping with the Bible's injunction, *The will of the Lord be done.* Acts 2:14

Egon was also agitated by Hitler's speech. "Hitler is well aware the German people have always been subservient to authority, Afra, and now he's created himself as the strong and powerful leader he knows they still want. But, Afra, for each of us to fulfill our greatest potential we must live the truth in our own heart – certainly not what some would-be dictator has in mind for us."

Hitler's crowds swelled to a hundred thousand, three hundred thousand – something the world had never seen. He shrewdly tapped into the people's discontent with the unstable government, the injustice of the Versailles Treaty, and unacknowledged anti-Semitism. With calculating deliberation he stirred up a fighting rage in the populace to gain increased support and financial backing from the German bankers.

Chapter 11

"This is a special day, Afra," said Egon. "A kind of graduation. You've studied diligently for two years and passed Froehling's tests for several branches of astrology: the natal horoscope, vocation, health, mundane, and predicting the future. You can see how all the elements of a horoscope fit together and come up with a comprehensive understanding. You also have a solid foundation of arithmetic and logic." He added one more thought, "And when you include your psychic ability with your astrological know how, you have a combination guaranteeing success."

"I believe it's time to open your own office." Egon looked at her expectantly.

She remembered her guardian angel's words and realized he was right. At last her dreams were coming true!

"You have such faith in me. If you think I'm ready to open my own office, then I am." She looked forward to making a living by helping people gain a better understanding of themselves and to glimpse into the future. By knowing when good fortune was about to strike, they could take advantage of new career opportunities, fortunate times for love and marriage, or a favorable time for an operation. If forewarned they could avoid an unhappy marriage, the first drink that might turn into an addiction, a trip that might end up in a tragic accident.

"Egon, I owe you so much. You taught me the spiritual side of astrology – and how to really love myself and others. And I want to start earning money so I can bring Ellen and Lilo to Berlin."

"You've come a long way, Afra. And so I have another idea!" A smile lit his face. "I know you've been anxious about your daughters. I agree that it's time to bring them here to be with you. I happen to be acquainted with an older widower that is looking for someone to stay at his place and help with housekeeping. His name is Herr Berger, and I assure you he has a very nice home. If you like, I'll be happy to speak to him about you."

She was elated. She knew she put on a brave front, but inside she desperately missed her daughters. It was hard to have no family life at all. Her smile was radiant. "How kind of you, Egon. It seems like I've been alone forever, and I really miss Ellen and Lilo."

Herr Berger was a small man in his early sixties with gray hair and a serious demeanor. "I can't pay for housekeeping," he told Afra, "but I'll allow you and your children to live here free. I know a number of people who put their trust in astrology. I'll send you clients, so you can make a living for your little family." Afra could hardly believe her good fortune. Eight days later she moved in her books and sparse wardrobe.

As soon as she was settled she returned to her parents to retrieve her daughters.

"Mutti, it's wonderful to be home!" she declared, basking in the familiar kitchen. She scratched the cat's tummy. "I missed the cat. I missed the coo-coo clock, the kettle boiling, and the wonderful smell of your cooking. But I especially missed you and Vater and the girls!"

"I cherish your visits, Afra."

"Me too. I can't begin to thank you for taking such good care of Ellen and Lilo."

Her mother set the tea on the table. "It will be lonely here when they go to Berlin. Their chatter and laughter liven up the place. In case you haven't noticed, being a mother and grandmother has been a big part of my life." She reached out and touched Afra's hand as she had so many times before. "Of course, there are always two sides to everything. Now I'll have time for myself." She studied Afra over her teacup. "But tell me, how are things going with you?"

"Oh Mutti, I feel as though I'm doing something I enjoy and that I do well. My astrology teacher says I'm a psychic spiritual astrologer."

"What more can a mother ask than to know her child is happy and fulfilled?"

Two days later Afra and her family were at the station, standing on the platform. The train appeared in the distance, slowed down gradually and came to a screeching stop. There were hurried hugs. Ellen and Lilo, caught up in the excitement of the crowd and the train trip, eagerly picked up their suitcases. Afra grabbed hers and steered them up the train steps. On the platform Mutti and Vater called out, "Auf wiedersehen, auf wiedersehen."

They found seats and hovered around the window. Her parents were waving. The next minute they were out of sight. Sinking back in her seat, she gave a sigh. Now she had to take on her responsibilities in full.

"Mutti," Lilo broke in to her thoughts, "can you help me find my book?" Together they pulled her suitcase off the rack. Lilo found her book. She settled into her seat again, one minute engrossed in reading, the next looking out the window at the passing countryside.

She could visualize Lilo's horoscope in detail. Like herself, Lilo was an Aries. She had the Moon in Libra. With this combination she wanted to be free and independent on one side, while on the other side she longed for love and emotional support.

When she didn't get her way she was prone to outbursts of temper. Usually Afra tried to appease her, while Ellen went along with her sister's bossiness.

Afra noticed Ellen had walked down to the far end of the car and was talking to a girl sitting by the aisle. Ellen was a Gemini with the Moon in Aries. She had such a pleasant, outgoing personality that she'd already made a friend. She was constantly on the move, like a bird ready to take off. But, like her father, she was restless, always looking ahead to new interests and challenges.

Afra imagined the girls all grown up, as loving wives and mothers as was her own mother, such a dear wonderful woman.

Two hours later the whistle blew and the train lurched to an abrupt halt.

"We're here!" exclaimed Ellen. They'd arrived in Berlin.

After a short drive their cab pulled in front of their apartment. "This is so different," exclaimed Ellen when Afra opened the door. "It's smaller than our house in Kassel, but it's a new adventure! Who knows what exciting things are going to happen here in the big city? Oh, look, Lilo," she cried as they entered their bedroom. "I love this wall paper with the yellow daisies! And the curtains are yellow, too. Very bright and cheery."

Lilo appraised the room, finally giving a look of satisfaction. "I'll take this bed," she said, plunking her suitcase on it.

It felt so good to have them with her again. Being away for so long made her love them even more.

They were happy in the little apartment. Her landlord helped care for Ellen and Lilo when Afra saw clients in her small office. She enjoyed the daily routine and soon everything was operating smoothly.

She never advertised. People came to her by word of mouth. She typed out each horoscope and tried to make everyone feel understood and supported. It was a satisfying experience connecting with a variety of people and their different personalities, interests and experiences.

It was a busy hard working time with much responsibility. Although she still longed to be a real writer, she was doing work she enjoyed within the framework of her family.

While Afra was busy establishing her astrological business, Hitler focused his energy on advancing his career with the Nazi party. Thanks to his efforts and outstanding organizational and speaking abilities, the once nonentity had become a formidable contender in the political arena.

Chapter 12

When Afra needed a larger place for her growing business, she found an apartment with a spacious office on Courbierestrasse, not far from Kurfuerstendamm. It had two bedrooms, living room, dining room, office, and steam heat.

She couldn't have been more pleased. Her new office was her sanctuary. On her desk were a telephone, a jar full of pens and pencils, and a tray overflowing with charts. Nearby a large file cabinet contained the horoscopes of her family, clients and famous people, as well as astrological notes from Egon's and Froehling's lessons. A bookcase held an ephemeris, table of houses, atlas and astrology books by Froehling, Heindel, Rudyar, Ebertin and other experts, past and present. She cherished those books, especially the old ones that championed ancient truths. Truths such as: "The basic pattern shown in your birth chart goes with you throughout life." And "The stars impel, but don't compel." When she read the words of wisdom she felt a connection with the astrologers who lived before her.

Afra and the girls happily settled in.

"Mutti," Ellen held out her pink satin toe shoes. "Can you sew ribbons on these for me?"

"Sure, Ellen," Afra pushed away the horoscope she'd been setting up and went to get her sewing basket. She sat down at the dining room table with her task, wondering why the manufacturers never sewed ribbons on toe shoes. Still, it pleased her that Ellen was ambitious to be a dancer. Afra always found time to take care of her children.

Ellen was fifteen years old: slender, light and graceful. Although she attended a sports school, it was the dancing part of the curriculum that drew her interest. She loved it all. The challenge of acrobatic tricks, the beauty of ballet, and the up beat rhythms of tap-dancing. Unlike ballet with toes pointed the instant they left the floor, in tap-dancing she learned how to relax her feet totally so the taps dropped off like raindrops – tippity-tap, tippity-tap, tippity-tap. She longed to make dancing her career and practiced the dance routines with her usual energy and high spirits.

Lilo was sixteen. The two girls were different in almost every way. Lilo was striking looking with raven colored hair that hung in thick waves to her shoulders. Her beautiful eyebrows arched over green eyes and high cheekbones. Ellen was a pretty girl — with blond hair, dark blue eyes, and boundless energy.

Afra and Lilo were in the kitchen getting dinner ready. Ellen was in the dining room setting the table when the doorbell rang. "Ellen, answer that," Afra called.

"All right, Mutti." Who could be calling at that time of the day? She set down the last fork and walked to the door. Opening it, she found herself staring at a pleasant looking woman holding a pot.

"Hello," said the stranger. "I'm Konstanze, your neighbor."

"Won't you come in?" Ellen greeted her. "What's that delicious aroma?"

"I brought you some Koniginpasteten." She held out a platter of patties bursting with meat filling.

"Oh, we absolutely love them! Let me call my mother."

Afra and Konstanze immediately hit it off. When Konstanze got to know Afra, she often managed to slip over to visit. Konstanze was definitely a people person.

Afra worked hard to form a profile of each client. They came for an annual forecast or to make an important decision. Romance and relationship questions were common. "Does he love me?" "Will we get married?" "Are we compatible?" She was always honest about what she read in the charts and picked up psychically. It was often very difficult for people to hear the truth concerning illness, death, unfaithfulness, divorce, financial ruin, and other weighty issues.

"She's my soul mate," a client explained with a lovesick look. "Of course we're going to get married, but I'd like you to do a marriage comparison chart for us anyway."

It was the worst comparison chart Afra had ever seen. He was an extroverted, unconventional Aquarian. She was an introverted, conventional Scorpio. Most of their planets squared each other, meaning a lot of exciting fireworks in the beginning, but plenty of conflict and disharmony later on. Against Afra's advice, they married. Six months later, the 'soul mates' got divorced.

During a reading for a client named Dustin, his horoscope revealed that as a child he had suddenly been separated from his father, as represented by the Sun in a T-Square with Uranus and Neptune.

Dustin said with a vigorous shake of his head, "No, no, Afra. Nothing like that has ever occurred. My father has always been there."

"It's interesting that you have secretive Neptune in the 4th House concerning a parent," Afra said. There's a skeleton in the family closet. Also, Uranus, planet of sudden separations, is in the 12th House of hidden things."

A month later, Dustin called. "Afra, you'll never believe this. I'm adopted. My father disappeared when I was a baby and my mother gave me up for adoption. I just found out."

Bernie was also known as "Bernadette" by his friends. Fascinated with astrology, he became a regular client. A female impersonator, he performed at the Cleopatra Cabaret. Cabarets had become popular in Berlin. The upper classes liked to eat, drink and dance all night. Erotic dancers, nude chorus girls and female impersonators were common. Prostitutes with boots and whips paraded the streets. Powdered and rouged young men sauntered along the elegant boulevards. The police ignored the decadence.

Bernie was handsome in a soft rather feminine way. He had plucked eyebrows that accentuated large liquid eyes and fine blond hair. Being in show business, his appearance played a leading role in his life. He defined his character with elegant pin striped suits, a silk handkerchief in his pocket and an exquisite ring on his little finger. His fans often showered him with chocolates in fancy boxes, putting weight on his hips; so he periodically went on crash diets.

Aside from his appearance and career choice, his horoscope clearly showed he was homosexual. Four planets were in Cancer: the Sun, Venus, Mars and Neptune. With Mars conjuncting erotic Neptune, he had an absorbing fantasy life and strange emotional desires. He was always involved in torrid love affairs, either flying high or crashing down into the abyss.

He treated Afra like the mother he wished he had. He brought her little gifts of flowers or chocolates. He invited her to be his guest at the Cleopatra.

Knowing he expected to see her all dressed up for the occasion, she asked Konstanze if she could borrow a couple of accessories. Konstanze, an artist at making everything beautiful, was delighted. White gloves, a pearl necklace and a jaunty little hat with a white feather more than satisfactorily complimented her simple black dress.

As her cab pulled up in front of the glitzy entrance of the cabaret, she was greeted by a huge black Senegalese doorman. His muscles bulged under a red jacket trimmed with brass buttons and epaulets trimmed in braid. He opened the taxi cab door, bowed formally, and with a flourish opened the huge glass door of the cabaret.

Afra was struck with stark contrasts of deep red and silver, the dominating colors of the cabaret. An elegant hostess in a black gown with a plummeting neckline led her to a table. A lamp with a red shade and a crystal ashtray decorated the black lacquered tabletop. Floor to ceiling mirrors reflected customers, waitresses and dancers.

A waiter brought her a bottle of champagne sent over by Bernie who was busy getting ready for his performance. She sipped her drink slowly. Looking around she saw the customers at the Cleopatra were an odd mix: the socially elite, military officers, adventurous sightseers, and unconventional swing kids. Lesbians and gay men lined the sweeping bar, checking everyone out and trying hard to emulate the opposite sex.

Suddenly everyone's attention was captivated by the sound of a drum roll and the band playing a rousing overture. A rotund master of ceremonies appeared in the pink spotlight and quickly warmed up the audience with some off-color repartee. When the laughter subsided, he announced: "And now what you've all been waiting for — the star of our show, Bernadette!"

Gowned, wigged and made-up, Bernie did impersonations of Greta Garbo, Marlene Deitrich and wisecracking singer-flapper Trude Hesterberg. He was an artist of illusion. Conversations and flirtations had stopped. Everyone was caught up in his magical spell. Amidst enthusiastic applause, he slipped behind a small screen. The drummer played a muffled beat. Everyone waited in anticipation. A hand snaked around the side of the screen. Then a woman with close cropped hair, dog collar, heavy leather bra, and skirt slit above the thighs appeared. At first Afra didn't realize it was Bernie.

"My name is Glinda Mash," the woman announced in a whiskey voice. "I will sing for you." The bass player struck a chord. She sang, "You are my sunshine, mein only sunshine. You make me happy" — suddenly, she swung out a whip and cracked it on the floor. "When skies are gray." Crack! The audience howled with laughter. As usual, Afra held a straight face. Suddenly she understood in that club with those people that it didn't matter what the neighbors or anybody else thought. Her face relaxed, her mouth twitched, she joined the laughter. Bernadette's act was outrageous.

Afra saw some ominous astrological warnings for Bernie. Coming up in 1933, progressed Mars would be squaring Neptune in his horoscope. "What does that mean?" Bernie asked.

"It means that someone will be taking secret action against you, and your life could be in danger. Please, Bernie, take me seriously. Thanks to the Nazi Party, things are getting worse here in Germany. I think it would be advisable for you to leave the country or at the least to give up your career for the whole of 1933."

Bernie, blissfully unaware of reality, shook his head. With naive confidence, he said, "My dear Afra, please don't alarm yourself on my account. Nothing like that will ever happen to me."

Chapter 13

In relaxed moments Afra started to have visions – piecemeal and vague at first, gradually becoming complete. She would find herself standing in her mother's kitchen, watching her cooking and taking care of other chores. Had she really been there, or was it just a fantasy? Other times she'd find herself in unknown places, looking at people, listening to conversations.

She asked Egon, "Do you know what's going on?"

"Why Afra," he said in surprise, "you're experiencing astral projection."

"What?"

"Let me explain. Having cleared yourself of much negativity plus your strong desire for greater awareness you are temporarily leaving your body and moving to distant locations in a non-material body.

The following week, Afra answered an unexpected knock on the front door. A distraught teenage boy stood before her.

"Frau Waesch?"

"Yes?"

"My name is Kruger. Please excuse me for coming without an appointment, but it's dreadfully important that I see you." His face bespoke a mixture of anxiety and fear.

"Come in, Kruger," she said as she closed the door behind him. Her hunches were becoming increasingly accurate and she asked without thinking, "Are you here about a missing man who drove a taxi?"

Startled, he answered, "Yes, Frau Waesch. It's my father. How did you know? He has been missing for a week, and I'm afraid something awful happened to him."

"Well Kruger, sit down. I think I may be able to find him." This was the perfect opportunity to see if she could teleport to a specific destination. With that in mind, she sat on the sofa, while he sat in a nearby chair, twisting his cap in his hands.

He looked like a nice boy – slim with that bony look boys have before they begin to fill out.

She said, "I'll lie here on the sofa and go into a special type of meditation that will help me find your father. Please pray with me." She could tell that Kruger hardly knew what she was talking about, but he was ready to try anything.

She lay down on the sofa. She closed her eyes. Her mind and body became still. Time slowed. Out of the silence, a roaring sound filled her ears. Bright lights flashed under her eyelids. Something shifted, and she realized she was floating upward, out of her body. It was an odd sensation, but she wasn't at all nervous. Focusing her thoughts on the young boy's father, she started to move quickly. It wasn't long before she stopped and found herself looking down at an abandoned taxi parked beside a barn. Kruger's father lay lifeless in a nearby wood. In the overhanging oak trees, birds twittered.

Her errand completed, she returned quickly to the apartment and rejoined with her body. As soon as she reoriented herself, she opened her eyes and sat up. "Kruger, I saw your father very clearly in a kind of vision. I'm afraid your worst fears are true. He was killed."

Kruger's breath caught. It was what he had dreaded all along. He wiped tears from his eyes, hardening himself to deal with the situation.

Afra described his father's appearance along with everything else she'd seen.

"How did you do that? You described my father perfectly! And I know the barn you were talking about."

Afra's voice was urgent. "You must call the police immediately and tell them that your father was murdered for his money. They will find his body in the snow. They will locate his remains today."

"Dankashen Frau Waesch," said Kruger as he left.

A few days later Afra opened the door. There, to her surprise, was Kruger back again. "Hello, Kruger. Please come in."

"Thank you, Frau Waesch," he replied as he entered the apartment. "I'm sorry to trouble you once more. The police found my father's body just as you described, but they have no idea who killed him."

"Well, Kruger, you caught me at a good time. I guess I should go into trance once more to see what we can discover. Please have a seat, and I'll lie on the sofa."

After a few minutes she found herself peering through smoky haze in a tavern. The room was noisy and filled with people, but her eyes were drawn to the figure of a man slumped over the bar. He sat with his head bent low, his elbows propped on the bar. His coat was lying on the stool next to him, and she saw scar tissue on his left arm where a tattoo of an anchor had been removed. Angrily he tossed his drink down his throat. He was the one who had murdered Kruger's father!

Upon traveling back into her body, she described her experience to Kruger. "This man works on a farm grooming horses. He's wearing a ring he took from your father. He has a tattoo of an anchor on his left arm that's partially hidden by a scar."

Soon after, Kruger came back once more to thank her and tell her that the police had located the man. "Frau Waesch, I had told the police my father's ring was missing, and that man was wearing it! He also had a tattoo like you described that he had attempted to remove. The police were able to see an anchor through the scar with a magnifying glass."

This time, when the boy left, he assertively put his cap on his head – a move that Afra felt sure meant he was assuming responsibility as a grown up.

Over time, astral travel became an integral part of her practice.

Chapter 14

Summertime arrived, sunny and bright. The girls were visiting Mutti and Vater for a couple of weeks. Most of Afra's clients were in the mountains or elsewhere for a break. She had time for herself. Picking up the phone, she dialed the number she knew so well. "Hello, Egon. Would you like to come over for dinner tonight?"

They had become good friends. She admired his brilliant mind and his depth. They had long discussions about astrology, metaphysics and world affairs.

Actually, she admitted to herself, she had a crush on Egon. It hadn't been an instant attraction. What she felt evolved over months of getting to know him, of knowing he was the only person who could see beyond her reserved façade. Not only did he understand her, he accepted her unequivocally. He wasn't dashing like Hagan, but attractive in a scholarly way and intellectually stimulating. She found herself caught up in romantic fantasies.

Of course she had plenty of other things to keep her busy, such as making a living and raising Ellen and Lilo. Also, ever since her divorce from Hagan, she was cautious about getting involved.

Seven o'clock Egon was at her door, flowers in hand. Surely it was going to be a perfect evening.

After the meal they moved to the living room. Afra placed a tray on the table by the sofa. "Help your self to sugar and cream," she said, handing him a cup of steaming coffee.

Absentmindedly Egon put a teaspoon of sugar in his cup. He was in a thoughtful mood. He noticed how much Afra had changed since he first saw her at Froehling's Astrology School. The unpleasant shades of color he'd observed in her aura were almost gone. And although she always held herself a little apart, she had hidden depths and great interior strength.

"Afra," he said, "many times I've stared at the piano, but nobody ever plays it. I think it's your piano. Could you make this a special evening and play for me?"

Playing the piano had always been a private satisfaction. She hardly understood it herself, but when she touched the keyboard all her inhibitions fled. Despite her hesitancy about playing for Egon, she sat at the piano. Her fingers lightly touched the keys, roaming up and down the scales. Music, more powerful than words could ever be, welled within her. Her restraints faded away. She spoke to him in resonant chords and surging arpeggios that flooded the room.

The passion and urgency of the music captured Egon. He came over and sat beside her. Watching her dancing fingers, he moved closer. When she felt his shoulder touch her, it was like an electric shock awakening something that had lain dormant. She looked at him over her shoulder. Their eyes met, and the joyful sound of the music swept them away.

He put his hand on hers, turned her toward him, and kissed her with an ardent tenderness she'd longed for.

Then her walls closed in. "I shouldn't be doing this," she whispered, wondering why it was so difficult to let go.

He touched his finger to her lips. "Shh, shh, my darling Afra. Don't you know how long I've loved you? Don't you know I would never hurt you?"

She couldn't move. As always happened, her stomach knotted up when it came to expressing her feelings. The problem was she cared for Egon too much. What if a deeper relationship ended up badly? "I've fallen in love with you," she whispered. She searched his eyes. "I'm afraid I'll disappoint you."

"I don't think that will ever happen. I know we'll be friends for life. Can't we be lovers, too?"

His voice was so tender. He held her face between his hands, searched it. There wasn't a trace of doubt between them. He pulled her closer and with infinite leisure kissed her, stroked her in unexpected places. The growing sensations transported her with delight. Caught up in an abandon she'd never known, she wrapped her arms around him and drew him to her. "I love you, I love you, I love you," she cried, the words pouring from her lips and her heart. He kissed her fervently, then pulled her up from the bench and led her into the bedroom.

With each passing week the bond between them deepened. He was always there for her, and she intuitively knew she stood solid in his heart forever. It gave her a sense of security she hadn't known before. She never worried that he was off with someone else.

Both she and Egon agreed they'd never get married. She was well aware that in her horoscope Mars, the planet of discord and strife, was in the 7th House of marriage. She could never forget all the fights, jealousy and emotional upsets when she was married to Hagan. And, while Egon was a wonderful companion, he had a private side. Their arrangement suited both of them.

~~

While Afra was blissfully happy in love, Hitler, despite his many female admirers, always had the feeling women were off-limits to him. In the back of his mind was a long ago memory of when he was a little boy and had put his hand on his mother's soft breast. "No, no, Adolph!" she had exclaimed in a shocked tone and pushed his hand away. "Never, never do that. It isn't proper." He was only a boy, and though she loved him dearly, she had wanted to instill the importance of conforming to correct behavior. "Always remember, Adolph, to be respectful in your conduct toward women." She had been stern, hoping her son would take her admonition to heart.

He had. His mother had no idea how much her rejection had hurt him or how terribly ashamed he was that he'd touched her. Sometimes he thought she didn't really love him. At other times he remembered all the dreadful beatings his father gave him, while his mother cringed in the corner, her beautiful eyes so full of love for him. He'd felt utterly helpless.

His father believed he knew what was best for everyone and ruled his family with a cruel, iron hand. Adolph's absolute refusal to submit to his demands that he follow him as a civil servant were met with explosive outbursts of anger and brutal beatings. Why must our family be so different from my friend Franz Kubizek? Adolph wondered. The Kubizeks were happy, always laughing and hugging each other.

He remembered the time when he was a teenager in love with the beautiful Stephanie. She was sixteen, a proper young lady, elegant and refined. For four years he had gazed at her longingly whenever she strolled down the Landstrasse. He had been so full of inferiority complexes and fear of rejection he couldn't approach her.

He didn't know why, but except for the untouchable Stephanie, he'd never longed for intimacy. When anyone tried to get too close his barriers closed in on him. "I have to concentrate all my efforts on my work," he claimed. His private life had been desolate and empty. He always held himself back. Masochism was the only way he could achieve even a degree of sexual satisfaction.

But with Geli things had been different. How she tantalized him! Her seductive ways and flashing eyes taunted him with an unspoken message: "I dare you." He had instinctively known she would be anything but inhibited, anything but proper. He felt that with her he could reveal hidden parts he had never dared acknowledge, even to himself.

Although Geli had plenty of male admirers, she relished being courted by her uncle, a man enveloped in an aura of power. She found him imposing with his knee length boots and the hippopotamus whip he carried coiled in his hand. Deftly she played on his debased erotic fantasies with overwhelming sexuality that both fascinated and shocked him. She reveled in the fact that Hitler had become her doting slave. She had a cruel, sadistic side that gratified his masochistic tendencies. He soon learned she would do anything, anything he asked – even beating him unmercifully with his whip. He would call out from the pain that was almost as harsh as the beatings his father used to give him while shouting, "Don't think for a minute you can disobey me, you no good worthless boy!"

Then suddenly, without warning his body would explode like a dam bursting over, releasing an indescribably exquisite force that electrified him from head to toe. He screamed out from the ecstasy of it, weirdly gratified being degraded by the woman he was obsessed with.

Geli calmly coiled up the whip and put it in the drawer. She lay down next to him – so remote he might have been alone.

Later, back in reality, he was keenly aware how much they were alike — ambitious, money-minded and calculating. He liked to show her off and took her everywhere – to meetings and conferences, to restaurants, cafes and theaters, on drives in the country, shopping for clothes. He wanted her only for himself and demanded she avoid the company of other men. If she went out without him she was chaperoned. She wanted to train to be a singer, but he wouldn't allow it. It was vital that he dominate her to maintain his sense of power and control.

Geli reacted to his unreasonable possessiveness with anger and an urge to get even. Their relationship was stormy. She revealed to a friend, "My uncle is a monster. Nobody can imagine what he demands of me." She hated his possessiveness, while at the same time relished the hold she had over him. However, the satisfaction she derived from the relationship was becoming overwhelmed with angry frustration. Unfortunately, she underestimated the extent of her lover's rabid possessiveness and jealousy. When she entered a room men were drawn to her high spirits and flirtatious glances. Blinding fury would seize Hitler's chest along with a growing conviction he could never really trust her. How could she behave that way after all he'd done for her? He angrily struck his palm with his whip. I could kill her, he thought, his brain gripped with murderous schemes.

He knew he had to pull himself together. What if he fell under one of his rages and lost control? It didn't bear thinking about. Geli was his and he couldn't let her go. He'd given her everything she wanted but she never seemed to appreciate it. Still, he was completely under her spell.

Knowing she especially loved expensive jewelry, he bought her an exotic Egyptian slave bracelet with entwined serpents. When he opened the door to her room, he was shocked to see her sitting on the bed in the arms of his bodyguard, ex-convict Emil Maurice. Overcome with rage, he'd flung the necklace at the startled couple. "Get out! Get out!" he screamed at Emil who quickly left.

Geli flung herself off the bed shouting, "I can't stand your tyrannical jealousy!" She angrily strode over to him. "Don't think for a minute you can control every area of my life. I'm not married to you! What makes you think you're my personal dictator?"

He almost lost control. His face became mottled and swollen with fury; he beat his fists on her chest. "How could you betray me like this? Don't you know yet that you are mine!"

He began seeing Eva Braun, his photographer's assistant. When Geli found out she was outraged. She flew into a blustery fit of temper, ranting to her housekeeper about her uncle's two-timing behavior. At last worn out, she stomped off and locked herself in her room. The next morning she didn't come down for breakfast.

There was no answer when the housekeeper knocked on the door. Worried, the woman called a locksmith. They found Geli lying on the floor, a pistol beside her. She had shot herself in the heart.

When Hitler got the news a look of frenzy covered his face. "How dreadful!" he cried, his voice rising almost to a scream. He retreated into his room, refusing to eat, pacing back and forth, hands clasped behind his back. He was unable to forget his niece and his magnetic attraction to her.

But after three days he rebounded from the depths of grief and returned to the only thing that brought him satisfaction, his obsession with power and total domination.

"I will get myself back together," he said to his photographer Heinrich Hoffman.

"I will take over power in Germany by 1933 at the latest. Now let the struggle begin – the struggle that shall be crowned with success."

He later confessed, "Geli was the only woman I ever truly loved."

Chapter 15

Afra hummed a melody to herself and shut the world out of her head. On that day nothing could quell her excitement about seeing Egon — her revered astrology teacher, dearest friend and wonderful lover.

She put on her warm woolen coat and felt hat. She wore her galoshes, as the afternoon's snowfall was melting and the streets would be clogged with dirty slush. Tucking her purse under her arm, she left the apartment. The few pedestrians looked as gloomy as the darkening sky: a girl pushing an old bike, a dozen Nazi soldiers wearing thick coats and heavy boots.

By the time she arrived at Egon's apartment, her cheeks were flushed and her breath accelerated, anticipating the evening that lay before her. But when Egon opened the door she saw distress in his eyes.

"What's the matter?"

"Wait," he said. He took her hand and led her down the narrow hall to the living room. They sat together on the sofa.

"Afra, I have some bad news. There was a report in the newspaper today that Willi had been 'unmasked as a dangerous enemy of the state.'"

She gasped.

"He was sent to Oranienberg concentration camp. The report said he had been 'shot during an escape attempt.' But I'm certain they murdered him there."

"No, Egon!" she cried in shock. "Hitler and his Nazis are terrible people, but why would they execute a sweet chap like Willi?" She felt sick inside. She reached out to Egon and held him in her arms. "Tell me what happened."

"The Gestapo probably had him shot. Afra, this is terrible." Egon stood up and began pacing back and forth in the small room as if to release his sorrow. "Willi was a capable astrologer and a talented writer and reporter. But he was too outspoken for these treacherous times. Once we were walking down the street together, and he said in a loud voice, 'Those Nazi fools. What on earth are they doing?' I warned him! But he just laughed. Someone must have reported him for such talk, including the fact he had many Jewish friends."

A minute ticked by on the clock. Although she hardly knew Willi, it was dreadful that such a thing could happen to an innocent young man. She said, "Do you remember when Willi told us astrologers not at the disposal of the Third Reich are kept under scrutiny by the Gestapo? Some are sent to concentration camps. Others are singled out for execution. They're never seen again."

Egon sat beside her once more. "Tragically, Afra, astrology isn't the safest profession in Nazi Germany."

"Who'll be next?" she asked. "Me? You? My children?" Little by little, the Nazis were curtailing her life.

Chapter 16

Afra's greatest wish was to bring the Light to humanity – to help people be their very best. But Hitler had a selfish design behind everything he did. He used trickery, misrepresentation and the Nazi Party to further his own empowerment. He declared to his fellow members, "In order to reach our goal we must use every means, even if we must work with the Devil!"

He was aware that to assume power he needed the support of the other Nazi leaders. To achieve this end, he had no qualms about using men that were street brawlers, murderers, bullies or sadists. He did have two basic requirements: absolute loyalty and unquestioning obedience.

Helpful in achieving his goals was Ernst Rohm, a skillful military commander with a special talent for drawing thousands of followers to Hitler and organizing them into Hitler's first strong-arm squads, later named Sturmabteilung or SA He effectively influenced the military and police authorities to protect and support Hitler's movement. Without Rohm's help, Hitler would never have gotten away with his brow beating and terrorist methods used to subdue his political opposition.

Rohm was an extremist. He worked hard and played hard. In his work he was disciplined, regimented, organized and exacting. If he deemed it necessary, he had no conscience regarding violence and murder. In his private life, he was probably one of the most wildly decadent Nazis. He flaunted his homosexuality and was driven to wanton pursuit of pleasure, sex and debauchery.

Rohm also gained the tolerance of the Army and the Bavarian government that helped Hitler carryout his tactics of intimidation and terror. At the same time Hitler was also cultivating bankers and influential industrial magnates whose financial backing made the Nazis the largest party in the government.

~~

January 30, 1933 -- Afra was wiping the dinner dishes when the announcement came over the radio. "Adolph Hitler has been appointed Reich Chancellor! Like a blazing fire, the news is spreading across Germany. A million hearts are aflame; a million hearts rejoice."

Hitler was exalted. Who would have dreamed the once failed painter would end up Chancellor, the highest official under President Hindenburg?

As Chancellor he had to submit to a certain amount of routine. However, he left as much as he could to others because he hated discipline and systematic work. His primary concern was to fortify his authority. He reversed the humiliating terms of the Versailles Treaty. He put his political opponents into concentration camps. He "protected" the people and State by suspending freedom of the press, the right to free speech and the constitutional guarantee of private property. He banned jazz, herded prostitutes into officially sanctioned brothels, and had homosexuals jailed or shot. Afra's friend Bernie mysteriously disappeared.

During the next few years he transformed Germany into a police state. He began by bringing the German states under his control, installing Nazi officials as their governors. He instigated a law that killed state parliaments and transferred all state powers to the central government. Next, to the satisfaction of his industrialist backers, he took over the labor unions.

Knowing the people expected solid material results, he got industry back on its feet again, created jobs for millions, and sponsored public works.

Almost everyone thrilled to the prospect of a resurgent economy and strong rearmament to command international respect. They failed to realize Hitler's real purpose was to drag them into another war in which he would be Germany's great hero.

The SA had grown to between two and three million men. Ever ambitious, Rohm wanted it to be the major military force in Germany, with the Army and Navy subordinate to it. He also wanted to be Minister of Defense. What Rohm didn't know was the industrialist financial backers and the Army refused to support Hitler if he allowed Rohm to take over the Army. Hitler needed both the Army and the industrialists' money to wage the war he was gearing Germany up for.

In the summer of 1934 there were rumors of a revolution, and in order to preserve his authority Hitler had to secure the Army's place as the sole armed force in the state. To accomplish this end he had, as usual, no scruples. He took care of dissident factions of the S.A by having over a thousand SA leaders executed.

Rohm was the only Nazi leader who had the guts to stand up to his friend Hitler. But Hitler never conceded to anyone.

Hitler realized everything would be ruined if the conflicts between Rohm and the Army and industrialists continued. Hitler's insatiable greed for power always came first. He had Rohm arrested and taken to Standelhelm Prison.

At first Rohm thought there must have been a mistake when he found himself locked up in a dismal cell with a bunk bed and bucket. Grayish light filtered in from a tiny window high up on the mortared wall. The air was dank with the smell of metal, mold, sweat, urine and feces. From time to time the silence was broken by screams from some part of the prison.

Reality hit. Rohm realized that Adolph had sacrificed him, his oldest and most loyal friend for ambition. He should have known, he thought, remembering Adolph's rage when he kept pushing him to consolidate the SA and the Army, with himself as Minister of Defense. He had also lost his temper with Adolph.

Hitler gave the order, "Leave a gun in his cell and give him ten minutes to kill himself."

A guard went to the prison and laid a gun on Rohm's bunk. In disgust Rohm turned away. When ten minutes were up, the door slowly opened. Two shots reverberated in the small cell.

One hundred men, perhaps two hundred, were executed without trial. The Nazi controlled newspaper, Volkischer Beobachter, and other papers hailed Hitler as a public hero for eliminating the terrorist element in the SA

~~

August 2, 1934 — President Hindenburg died at age 87. It was announced that a law enacted the preceding day combined the offices of Chancellor and President and that Hitler had taken charge as the head of state and Commander in Chief of the Armed Forces. The title of President was discarded, and Hitler would be known as Fuhrer and Reich Chancellor. He had all military officers and men swear an oath of unconditional obedience to him until death. His dictatorship was complete. He, and only he, had total control.

Chapter 17

With uncanny shrewdness born of the Moon and Jupiter in Capricorn, Hitler revived the ancient custom of torchlight parades that Germans loved. The rousing military music and endless line of bobbing torches stirred long held instincts of the German people.

Afra, along with Konstanze, her husband Gustav, and their son Freddie, stood on the sidewalk waiting for the big parade. A noisy crowd surrounded them on all sides. Above, people were leaning out of windows and over balconies. Red flags and strips of cloth emblazoned with black swastikas rippled and snapped in the breeze.

Freddie stretched forward as far as he could, anxious for the marching, the music and the singing to begin. But most of all, he wanted to see the Hitler Youth in the parade. The Fuhrer had won over millions of German children and organized them into well disciplined Nazis. The boys in the Youth Group enjoyed hiking, camping and sports and were instructed in shooting, flying and other requirements of war.   They were taught to fight for Germany and, if necessary, to die for Germany.

Freddie tugged on his father's hand. "Listen!" he cried. In the distance came the sound of a band, just like the military music of the Great War. As it grew louder, a feeling of exhilaration swept through the crowd. Freddie was so excited he could hardly stand still.

First, they saw the drum and fanfare platoon followed by hundreds of boys marching in formation.   They were smartly dressed in uniforms much like Hitler's Storm Troopers: brown shirts, black ties, black shorts and white knee socks. Daggers were strapped to their belts and armbands bore the Nazi swastika inside a white diamond on a field of red and white. In a chorus they sang, "Germany belongs to us today; tomorrow it will be the world." Hitler's Storm Troopers marched behind them.

Then Hitler came into view standing in an open black Mercedes touring car. This was the first time Afra had seen him close up. It was amazing to her how such a common looking man with his stiff salute could unleash such hysterical acclaim. Freddie and his parents joined the crowd. "Heil Hitler!" they shouted and raised their arms in salute.   Afra, fearful of consequences, reluctantly lifted her arm.

She knew the military music, scores of marchers, brightly colored swastika banners, and fancy car were just extravagant trappings. Hitler wanted everyone to see him as the strongest, the greatest and most powerful leader Germany had ever known. He wanted to be the center of attraction with all eyes focused, adoringly upon him.

All Afra could think of were the dismal portents in his horoscope.

Hitler acknowledged the delirious welcome with a thin smile, still holding his outstretched arm. Some women looked as though they might swoon.   The crowd's extravagant enthusiasm was infectious.

Freddie's childish face expressed the parade was far beyond his expectations.

The next day, Konstanze told Afra, "I tried to dissuade Gustav from allowing Freddy to join the Hitler Youth, but he already told Freddie he could."

"I was afraid of that," Afra said.

Konstanze added, "Hitler has taken those children and brainwashed them into blind obedience. I think he duped them and just about everyone else with all the pageantry, fanfare and false promises. Der Fuhrer comes first — before family, friends and God."

Afra said, "He pretends to work for the people, but everything is for his own personal power. He'll use the children for whatever he needs — spying on their parents, farming or digging trenches."

Konstanze shook her head, "You're right of course, and Gustav says any parent who tries to keep a child from joining could be sent to prison."

A year later at age ten, Freddie was sworn into Jungvolk, the junior branch of the Hitler Youth. He made an oath to give his life to Hitler and the Fatherland.

Konstanze and Gustav had less and less influence over him.

From the very start the Hitler Youth leaders built on the premise the boys had already learned in school – that a leader must be obeyed unconditionally, even if it seemed harsh, punitive or unsound. They were told it was the only way to avoid chaos.

Chapter 18

Three weeks after Ellen graduated from school, she was limbering up with dozens of other dancers auditioning for "Strength for Happiness," a huge Nazi spectacle to encourage physical fitness and inspire a sense of national pride in Germany's youth.

While going through her stretches she chatted with Yvonne, a stunning blond with peaches and cream skin. Vivacious by nature, Yvonne was blessed with a down to earth wholesomeness. She told Ellen she had worked with an act that had recently broken up.

"What do you think our chances are?" asked Ellen, a bit nervous at her first audition.

"Personally, I dislike 'meat inspection' auditions. It's so easy to get lost in the shuffle — the producers and choreographer become exhausted auditioning so many people. Sometimes they cut a dancer short after doing one grand jeté' or a singer after singing only one phrase." She noticed a frown on Ellen's face.

"But don't worry. In show business luck is a factor." She smiled encouragingly, "You never know what might strike their fancy."

Finally the door to the rehearsal hall opened. The dancers who'd already auditioned streamed out. A man called, "We're ready for dancers with numbers twenty-one through thirty."

Ellen, Yvonne and the rest of the dancers entered the room. The choreographer's assistant led them through a vigorous athletic combination. Putting her trepidation aside, Ellen absorbed herself totally in the dance, the music, and smiling brilliantly for the small audience of men seated at the front. Sixteen girls were thanked and excused; Ellen, Yvonne and the remaining dancers were told they would be notified for a call back.

Opening the dressing room door, they were greeted with the sound of dozens of dancers chatting and laughing and a mixed smell of perspiration and cologne. "Let's see, I'm locker 54," said Ellen as she made her way to a rickety locker. Yvonne found hers on the other side of the room. They changed into their street clothes.

"I'm glad that's over," said Yvonne when they walked out of the building. "Let's grab a bite to eat."

Over, a bowl of pea soup Ellen asked, "What kind of an act were you working with?"

"Well, I'm a coloratura soprano. I can hit a high C quite easily. I performed with a huge concert troop. When we played here in Berlin we had a ninety-man orchestra. I can't begin to tell you what it was like to hear the music swell through the theater, surround me and transport me with heavenly sound."

"It must have been incredible," Ellen agreed. "I know that even a small group of live musicians is better than recorded music. Did you work with any opera stars?"

"Oh, yes! I worked with Ericka Blomberg and quite a few others." Yvonne took a hungry bite of bread. "Guess why all those opera singers are so fat?"

"I haven't a clue."

"Well, to have good volume and sustain notes, they need a lot of food to pump air up from the stomach. They are given double food stamps. Workers complain. Why should anyone need more food just to stand up on a stage and sing?"

Ellen let out a peal of laughter. "So why aren't you with the concert group now?"

"Because the tours are seasonal. Also, since I dance as well as sing, I thought I'd try something different."

In many ways, Ellen and Yvonne were very much alike, hard working, happy, and fun loving. They enjoyed each other's company and began exercising together.

"Ellen," Yvonne said while they sat on a bench at a rehearsal hall, "I'm really getting in shape working out with you." She began wiping perspiration off her face. "Do you know, ever since the act broke up my agent has been urging me to work as a single. But I don't want to work alone." Inspired, she grabbed Ellen's hand and pulled her in front of the mirror. "See how good we look together. Why don't we create a new act? I think we'd make a good team."

Ellen beamed with the thrill of doing an act with Yvonne, someone she really liked and who was a talented and experienced professional.

"Now," cried Yvonne, "let's see how we look dancing together. We'll do the old soft shoe."

They sang, "Give me the old soft shoe; I said the old soft shoe."

"Ah 1," sang Yvonne.

"Ah 2," sang Ellen.

"A doodley, oodley do," they sang in perfect harmony. They danced the familiar soft shoe steps.

"Can't you see us, Ellen, in black satin leotards with black net tights, top hats and white tipped canes?"

Ellen was already imagining them tapping away to the applause of a big audience.

She was excited and caught up in Yvonne's idea. She found herself thinking of rehearsals, new costumes and orchestrations. Also, they should have a gimmick, something different.

They started rehearsing and it wasn't long before their act was ready. They called themselves the Dana Sisters and performed at many places, including the famous Moulin Rouge in Paris. The Parisians loved them and referred to them as the second Dolly Sisters.

Their most popular number was "Deux Femmes de la Chambre" about two French chambermaids. Ellen cart-wheeled on stage in a theatrical French maid costume: black with puffed sleeves and a short ruffled skirt. Her dainty apron was a most impractical affair, as were her high-heeled shoes. She pranced about dusting everything with a pink feather duster. Her routine included high kicks, dazzling acrobatic walkovers and a split. Dust, dust, dust.

Yvonne appeared, a saucy nose-in-the-air maid with a sexy walk. She gingerly held a full tray with a coffee pot, sugar bowl, cup and saucer. As she strutted across the front of the stage, suddenly she tripped in a clumsy pratfall. The people seated in front screamed and leaped out of the way as dishes, coffee, cream and sugar went flying. But there was Yvonne holding her tray with everything in place as before. The paper mache dishes were attached to the tray with strings and the sugar and cream were actually bits of confetti. The audience ate it up. The Dana Sisters routinely received encore after encore after each performance.

The two friends toured the cabaret and vaudeville circuit, appearing with comics, hand balancing acts, jugglers, singers and dog acts. They enjoyed every moment. "Look, Ellen!" cried Yvonne holding up a thick letter backstage at their latest cabaret booking. "It's a contract from our agent, Herr Schmidt. He's booked us at the Café der Comica on Kurfurstendamm. We're going back to Berlin to work in Germany's fanciest cabaret where the most famous comedians and entertainers appear!"

"Whoopee!" cried Ellen, and they locked elbows, dancing in circles of joy.

The Café der Comica was sumptuously decorated with gold plated chandeliers. Huge original paintings of old masters lined the red velvet walls. Customers chatted at little round tables, while waitresses served drinks.

It was a showcase of fashion, the most expensive popular place for the upper class and high-ranking Nazis. The men wore beautifully cut tuxedos, made-to-order dress shirts and carried pencil thin gold cigarette containers. The women were dressed in elegant evening gowns, fur coats and stoles, and abundant jewelry. Carefully premed and made-up with arched eyebrows and crimson lipstick. Many held long cigarette holders in gloved hands, like Marlene Deitrich, screen idol of the day.

Ellen and Yvonne, having finished the late show, were in their dressing room shedding their costumes and washing up at a sink. "Ellen," asked Yvonne, "did you see that fat man in the front row?"

"How could I help it?" She let out the laughter she'd been holding in since she first saw the overstuffed man in his ostentatious, large labeled uniform, a gold braid lanier looped from an epaulet, and a chest full of medals,

"Ellen, don't you know who that is?"

"No, should I?"

"That's Herman Goring. I guess you didn't notice, but among those medals was the famous Pour le Merite."

Ellen nodded, "Oh, now I know who he is. Mutti told me that Goring is Hitler's second man and the richest man in Germany. He has a palace here in Berlin and a 700,000 acre country estate. He's supposed to be a big hunter. His estate is supplied with gamekeepers, wardens, servants and plenty of deer. I really can't stand people that flash around their so-called importance!" She gave her hair a vigorous brushing.

"Rich or not, Goring's nothing but a brute." Yvonne zipped up her sparkling evening dress. "Nobody says 'No' to him." She reached for an earring. "There's a thousand ways he can get even." She put on her other earring. "Permits cancelled, jobs in jeopardy, parents attacked."

She was applying her lipstick when they heard a knock on the door. Ellen peeked out. "Excuse me, ladies," said one of the many waiters. "Herr Goring requests the pleasure of your company at his table."

The two girls looked at each other in shock – not such a good idea to say 'No.' "Please thank him for us," said Yvonne. "We'll join him in a few minutes."

As they walked through the cabaret, they drew envious glances from the women and open admiration from the men. It was easy to spot Goring. Ruddy cheeks and a lascivious grin sat upon his mountainous body. His effusive voice greeted and invited them to sit, one on each side. Ellen found it hard to believe he was the once trim fighter pilot, a hero of the Great War, whose picture had been splashed across the newspapers.

Ogling the girls, he introduced them to his party: a millionaire industrialist, a famous Olympic athlete and three bob-haired young women beautifully slinky in satin gowns.

Ellen's bubbly conversation and Yvonne's dynamic presence fit right in. Ellen had to admit their host was entertaining with his flamboyant genial personality and sense of humor. She came back to reality after he whispered a couple of vulgar sexual innuendos. Then someone mentioned that her mother was a well known astrologer. She hoped Goring wasn't paying attention.

In parting, he gave her an autographed picture and stared at her cleavage again. She felt violated, almost as if he had thrown her on the floor and raped her.

The next morning Mutti went to the front door and picked up a bag of bakery fresh buns hanging on the doorknob. She took them to the kitchen where Ellen sat reading the newspaper.

"How about hard boiled eggs for breakfast, Ellen?"

"Thanks, Mutti." She looked up and put the paper away.

Afra put the warm eggs under their own little cozy and placed them with the buns on the table. She sat down with Ellen. "Now tell me about your booking at the legendary Café der Comica."

Ellen appreciated her mother's interest in her career. "Everyone loved our act, Mutti. Herr Schmidt has lined up a few more bookings. A lot of well-known people were at the café, including Herman Goring. He all but propositioned me. The fat pig. He's got an exaggerated opinion of his importance and was bent on impressing everyone." She paused to spread butter and honey on a bun. Then her thoughts returned to Goring, and she took a vicious bite. "Mutti, there's something about his eyes – a gigantic hunger."

As soon as Afra finished her breakfast she went to her office to get Goring's horoscope. It annoyed her that he had clouded Ellen's sunny smile. She returned to the kitchen and propped his chart up on her coffee cup. "Goring is a greedy man, Ellen. He's an ambitious Capricorn, and his Moon in Scorpio signifies extravagant materialistic desires. He wants power and an unending stream of indulgences and possessions."

She vigorously wiped a greasy spot from the linoleum tablecloth. "Unfortunately, people are usually taken in by his powerful magnetism and expansive personality. Underneath there's always some ulterior motive."

Ellen gave an involuntary shudder when she recalled sitting next to him.

Afra spoke in a tone that underlined her concern. "I sincerely hope you don't run into him again. Although he appears to be a man of good will, he's one of Hitler's killers in charge of executions. I wouldn't want you to know him even casually. He might try to win you over by getting you dancing engagements."

They talked of other things. The atmosphere lightened. Afra knew there were some awful men in that group of Nazis. She couldn't help but be concerned about Ellen and Yvonne.

Chapter 20

Afra was worried about Germany's economy and began checking on the prices of commodities like soap, toothpaste, milk and sausages. As she suspected, there'd been a steady increase in prices ever since Hitler first came to power. Cooking fat and several other items had gone up fifty percent. At the same time, the quality of almost everything had gone down, and awful artificial foods like coffee made mostly with chicory were becoming regular staples. Instead of improving the economy, Hitler was raising taxes and demanding 'voluntary' contributions for his vast building projects and his so called peacetime army of 550,000 men. Amazingly, the great powers hardly protested this violation of the Versailles Treaty.

Afra wasn't the only one concerned about the economy. Haljamar Schacht, Hitler's Minister of Economics, had devised some clever schemes that raised money for Germany's military buildup and helped pay the armament bills. However, as early as

1936 he'd warned Hitler that Germany was approaching the limit towards near bankruptcy.

As usual, Hitler did things his own way, and he instructed Goring accordingly.

In 1938 Goring declared to the Reich Defense Council, "Even though our economy is showing signs of strain, we must concentrate all our resources on raising the level of rearmament. Everything must be subordinated to this single task." When Schacht protested against that reckless expenditure, Hitler handed him his dismissal.

Hitler commissioned his architect Albert Speer to rebuild Berlin on a grandiose scale. "These buildings," he told him, "are to tower up like cathedrals in the millennia to come. They will be so gigantic even the pyramids will pale before the masses of concrete and colossi of stone I am erecting here."

Speer drew up plans and began ordering huge quantities of granite purchased from Sweden, Norway and Finland. To bring it to Berlin, he organized transport fleets and shipyards with plans to build 1,000 boats with a capacity of 500 tons each.

Hitler's colossal building plans were only one facet of his insatiable greed and self-aggrandizement. He ordered the building of a new and massive Chancellery. He kept a fleet of automobiles, and airplanes at his disposal. He collected rare paintings, engravings and books. Servants and secretaries were at his beck and call.

Chapter 19

The main purpose of the SS (formerly Storm Troopers) was the extermination of opponents of the Third Reich, real and imagined. After he seized control of the government, Hitler appointed Heinrich Himmler SS Reichfuhrer and chief of the dreaded Gestapo. Himmler was fascinated with astrology and the occult and became head of a top secret intelligence unit called the Nazi Occult Bureau.

The Bureau had thirty astrologers on duty twenty-four hours a day using astrology, psychic phenomena and other occult sciences to help win the war. They used astrology to calculate auspicious times, mental telepathy to influence the enemy, pendulum dowsing to locate enemy ships. They airdropped leaflets with revised predictions of the 16th Century seer/astrologer Nostradamus to make it appear Germany was going to win the war.

In turn, the British had their own secret units with pendulum dowsers and astrologers who foretold Hitler's favorable and unfavorable times. They, too, airdropped slanted astrological interpretations.

Lord Tweedsmuir, better known as the novelist John Buchan, warned politicians about the covert occult practices of the Nazis and the kind of world domination that could emerge from German technology combined with Black Magic. His warnings were ignored. It was impossible for most people to admit the satanic nature of the Nazi Party.

~~

Afra looked out the window. The weather was cold and dreary. She thought it might rain. Lightning flashed against a background of darkening clouds. Behind her she heard the phone ring. "Frau Afra Waesch?

"Yes, I'm Frau Waesch."

"This is Gestapo Headquarters. You're directed to come to Reichfuhrer Himmler's office immediately. We will expect you within the hour."

"Oh — I'll leave right away," she said, worrying what they could possibly want with her. She recalled that after Ernst Rohm was killed, Himmler and his SS used their almost limitless power in frightening ways. She dressed quickly, ran her comb through her hair, and applied a touch of lipstick. She put on her coat and hat, grabbed her umbrella, and left the apartment.

Outside the sky had darkened and rain began falling in torrents. The weather is as depressing as my mood, she thought as she buttoned her coat and opened her umbrella. Still, the rain was refreshing and she was feeling more optimistic by the time she stepped off the tram for her appointment with the SS Reichfuhrer.

When she entered Himmler's office, he rose from behind his desk and walked over to her. He studied her carefully. She was a rather plain woman, but reputed to be a remarkable astrologer. Ordinarily he would have called on one of his own astrologers, but Frau Waesch was said to be highly skilled at setting a favorable time for serious operations and he wasn't going to take any chances. Greeting her politely, he led her to a chair and seated himself behind an ordinary desk set in front of a blank wall.

Afra watched him curiously. He was a homely man with a pallid complexion, trim moustache, receding chin and narrow shoulders. Thick glasses magnified his eyes. Although he wore a meticulously tailored uniform, he looked like a common office clerk. Despite his unimpressive appearance, Afra knew he was a dangerous man associated with concentration camps and mass murder. She also knew his agents were cracking down on astrologers, fortune-tellers and other esoteric practitioners outside of the Occult Bureau who were suspected of making astrological predictions unfavorable to Hitler or the progress of the war. She was sure he was behind Willi's death.

Nervously pulling a cigarette out of a pack he spoke in a quiet voice with a slight Bavarian accent. "I've studied astrology a bit myself, Frau Waesch, and it's my understanding that it's possible to set a propitious time for an event, a time when the planets are harmoniously placed."

She wondered what he was leading up to. She said, "Not only is it possible for us to predict the future, Reichfuhrer Himmler, but we also help our clients choose favorable times for important happenings."

"Frau Waesch, I have excruciating headaches." He pressed his fingers to his brow. "The doctors have done extensive tests, but have no idea what's wrong. I've had a tendency towards illness my whole life, and I'm worried these headaches may be an indication of something really serious. I've heard you have exceptional astrological acumen. I would appreciate it if you could diagnose what's wrong, and if I need an operation to set a time for it."

An image flashed in her mind — Himmler dies during the operation and she, the scapegoat, is standing in front of an SS firing squad with rifles aimed at her.

She took a slow breath, "Yes, I can do that. I'll need your birth date, place of birth and the exact time."

Himmler stubbed out his cigarette. He gave her the information she required and thanked her profusely as he escorted her to the door.

Afra calculated his horoscope as soon as she got home. He had the Sun in Libra. In that position the Sun's vitality was somewhat weakened. The Moon was in Aries that rules the brain, and made a close T-Square with Saturn and Neptune. This difficult configuration was slowing down the functioning of his brain and causing some kind of poisonous deposit. She knew the cause. Tumors were ruled by the Moon, and his Moon was badly afflicted in Aries. She was certain he had a brain tumor.

It was obvious to Afra that Himmler had a badly conflicted horoscope, and she knew there was a strong connection between the mind, emotions and body.

As was often her habit, she glanced at his chart then closed her eyes to psychically tune in to his childhood. She saw his parents' annoyance at their clingy weepy child. For heaven's sake, crying and tender heartedness was unmanly — a clear admission of weakness. They drummed into Heinrich and his brothers the importance of outward appearance and to follow rules and regulations. As a result of his emotionally stifled childhood and parental demands for perfection, he grew up with an underlying fear of inadequacy all shown by his T-Square.

To offset this, the Grand Trine between the Moon, Mars, Jupiter and Uranus enabled him to cultivate a show of confidence and hardness, unflinching determination to overcome difficulties, and powerful leadership and organizing ability.

His chart appeared to be a morass of conflictions, hard and cruel on one side, and strongly tied to his emotions on the other.

Once more Afra closed her eyes. Her psychic vision revealed an image of Himmler crying at the sight of SS brutality. He was constantly at war with himself as a result of his heinous crimes against humanity at Hitler's behest.

His doctors must have suspected the tumor but claimed they didn't know to avoid retaliation in case he died. She was the one to be held responsible if the operation failed. If only she could run away and leave Germany and all its troubles. She looked longingly out the window. How she would have loved to set up an unfavorable time for the operation to rid Germany of an evil and destructive man.

Perhaps it was her Christian upbringing, but she couldn't do it. Therefore she returned her attention to her work. Carefully she calculated a time for his operation, rechecking again and again. A tiny mistake could be fatal for the Reichfuhrer. Even worse, it could be fatal to her. Finally satisfied, she placed a phone call to the Gestapo and was immediately connected with Himmler. She gave him her diagnosis and a favorable date and time for the surgery. "Reichfuhrer Himmler, although you will be in a coma for three days after the operation, the surgery will be a success," she assured him.

Two hours later his secretary called her back and asked her to be present during the surgery the following day. She knew that she was going to be held captive in case anything went wrong. Although Ellen and Lilo did their best to put on a brave face, she could tell they were sick with fear. That night she was unable to sleep; it was impossible to keep from worrying. By the time the day for Himmler's surgery arrived, she was exhausted.

A burly SS soldier came for her. He told her to pack her clothes; she was to stay at the Chancellery until the Reichfuhrer recovered. She threw a few things in a suitcase and hugged the girls. Nobody cried, but it was a tense farewell. She wasn't sure if she'd ever see them again. The soldier drove her to the hospital and took her to the waiting room. The operation took forever. As she had predicted, Himmler came out of the anesthesia but remained in a coma.

She was installed in comfortable quarters. Strangely, she became very calm. Three days later Himmler woke from the coma. The doctors declared the surgery a success, and she was released to go home.

Chapter 21

A week later Afra got a call from Hitler's office. "Frau Waesch," the woman announced, "The Fuhrer requests your presence at his villa in Bavaria. You will be picked up at nine in the morning tomorrow. Please bring an overnight bag."

What was going on? All of a sudden so much interest from the Gestapo, Himmler, and now Hitler? "Oh, of course," she answered. "Can you tell me the purpose?"

"I'm sorry, Frau Waesch, I do not know. However, he asks that you bring your ephemeris and charts." With that the woman hung up the receiver.

When Afra arrived at the villa, Hitler was still asleep. Eva Braun, his mistress, greeted her. Afra had been looking forward to seeing the mountains, so Eva took her and Eva's two dogs on a long walk through the grounds. The mists slowly cleared revealing the distant mountain peaks against a deep blue sky.

Hitler was a late sleeper. It was two in the afternoon by the time he joined them for a relaxed lunch, following which Afra and

Hitler were driven along frightening hairpin turns to his occult hideout, Eagle's Nest. About a mile from the villa they pulled up beside a mountain. It was no ordinary mountain. Cut into the side was an unobtrusive door that led to a sloping underground passageway. As they walked, the silence became oppressive. There was something gloomy and heavy about the atmosphere – a foreboding sense of evil. Finally they came to an elevator with two bronze doors. Hitler pressed a button, the doors slid open, and they were soon moving up a 6,000 foot shaft drilled through the heart of the mountain.

Afra reflected on Hitler's extravagances amidst the shortages she and everyone in Germany were experiencing.

Perched on the mountain's summit, Eagle's Nest was an observatory that revolved 360 degrees around to give an unobstructed view of the heavens. However, it was consigned to astrology rather than astronomy.

"I call this room the Chamber of Stars," said Hitler proudly. Astrological symbols were painted on the walls, and the Zodiac was pictured on a high ceiling of deep blue glass. Hitler pressed a switch and the planets moved. "You see, Frau Waesch," he explained, "my astrologers can adjust the aspects of the stars mechanically to the latitude and longitude at any given place and moment.

"This is where my personal astrologer and his team calculate the stars and make forecasts that enable me to take advantage of the most favorable times in government affairs, foreign policy and military offenses."

Afra was boggled by the effort and money Hitler put into his narcissistic quest for power.

He showed her a second room for treasure mapping on a grand scale. At one end, a semi-proscenium arch framed a series of photographs from a slide projector. They were much more than ordinary photographs, technically beautiful yet misleading photo-montages with one photograph superimposed on another.

"What's the purpose of it?" Afra asked.

"For example," Hitler explained, "take this montage dealing with Czechoslovakia. These pictures deal with all phases of life in that country." He marked them off on his fingers: "Industrial, business, banking, military, farming, school, street and home scenes." Through modern photography, symbols of Nazi occupation were superimposed. Nazi flags and banners replaced Czechoslovakian flags, and there were pictures of Hitler riding in parades on the main streets of Prague and Nazi soldiers strolling down streets. Photographs of Hitler hung on the walls of homes. All looked as though Czechoslovakia was already occupied by the Nazis. The pictures blended into one with the date March 14 when all this was to become an accomplished fact.

"These montages," Hitler continued, "are thrown on the screen with regularity and viewed by a group of men using visualization, affirmations and projection."

"But why am I here?" asked Afra.

"Please have a seat, Frau Waesch." They sat on two comfortable looking chairs. "Reichfuhrer Himmler has acquainted me with your expertise, and I would like to see if you concur with my astrologers. Do you foresee anything significant coming up for me?"

Afra always kept up to date on Hitler's charts and she drew them out of her briefcase. "Actually, I do. I'm sure your astrologers have informed you that you are currently under two favorable influences for 1938 and 1939. Progressed Venus is trining your natal Jupiter, signifying phenomenal good luck. Progressed Sun trining natal Uranus means dynamic leadership, surprising plans and unexpected ventures are producing spectacular results."

Hitler smiled with satisfaction. "That's proved true so far. As you know, my troops have successfully marched into Austria."

Afra nodded, and then put up her hand. "On the other side, transiting Pluto is squaring your Sun until the middle of 1941. While Pluto is the smallest of all the planets, it's the most powerful and the most fixated. If you should become obsessive in a drive for power, you would exceed your boundaries and meet with overwhelming opposition." Before she could continue further, Hitler jumped to his feet, his face contorted in rage. "That will be all, Frau Waesch." His voice was cold as ice. He picked up the phone and called his chauffer to take her back.

March, 1939 – The League of Nations did nothing when Hitler took over the Rhineland, Sudentenland, Austria and Czechoslovakia. They had no means to enforce their decisions.

April 20, 1939 – Bells pealed at swastika-bedecked churches, summoning Hitler's people to the observance of his birthday and his triumphant takeover of Austria and Czechoslovakia. To signal the importance of this day, the National Socialist government granted German workers a paid holiday, guaranteeing a huge turnout for the greatest military spectacle ever staged.

At 11 a.m. Hitler walked to his waiting black convertible. Frowning at the overcast sky, he willed the clouds to open, the sun to break through. They motored down the majestic new Via Triumphalis, preceded by motorcycles with yellow standards fluttering from their windshields. This is my day, he thought, as he stood in the car, soaking in the deafening cheers of the huge crowd. They pulled up by the reviewing platform where he joined the chiefs of staff, generals, field marshals and admirals. Behind them hovered a gigantic German eagle and six swastika banners.

For over four hours Hitler stood at attention while 40,000 members of Wehrmacht's troops goose-stepped down the boulevard, accompanied by horse cavalry, anti-aircraft guns, tractor-drawn cannon, and over 100 tanks. For the grand finale Goring's Luftwaffe soared above. But somewhat marring the great show of German power, the sky remained dark and leaden.

August 31, 1939 -- Hitler was in a state of high excitement. His lightning blitzkreig attack on Poland was going to come off the next day.

"My Fuhrer," asked Albert Speer, "may I show you an idea I have for the enormous domed building you've been considering?"

Hitler nodded and Speer brought out a sketch. "There high on top of the dome I put the German eagle with the swastika in its claws."

Speer saw by the faraway look in his Fuhrer's eyes that he had an idea of his own.

Hitler drew himself tall and spoke to an imaginary audience that stretched beyond the walls of his office. "Instead of the swastika to crown the greatest building in the world we must have the eagle standing above the globe."

September 1, 1939 – Definitely into his Fuhrer mode, Hitler grappled with crucial military decisions and ordered surprise attacks with total self-assurance. German armies poured across the Polish frontier, destroying the Polish Air Force and vanquishing the Polish Army. Ancient German land once more came under German rule, and Hitler was surrounded by triumphant soldiers. Some of the injustices of the Versailles Treaty were vindicated.

September 3, 1939 – Britain and France declared war on Germany. They finally realized Hitler was not so much interested in reclaiming German territory as in using the Versailles Treaty as an excuse for a policy of expansion.

By the end of the day, India, Australia and New Zealand had become part of the Allied force against the Third Reich. The German people were in a state of shock. Hitler had led them into another war.

May, 1940 – Hitler had conquered Czechoslovakia, France, Denmark, Norway, Holland and Belgium. With over one hundred million Europeans under his rule he was master of the new German empire that extended from the Atlantic Ocean to the Volga River and from the Artic Circle to North Africa. He proved he was the greatest of all Germans. Still, he was haunted by a foreboding that the evil spirit that visited him when he viewed the Spear of Destiny would some day demand a price for the supernatural powers he had bestowed on him.

Despite Hitler's spectacular victories, production output in his arms manufacturing industries all over Europe began falling sharply because of slave labor sabotage and the near exhaustion of food supplies that reduced workers' efficiency. By autumn the yield of German industries leveled off and kept dropping.

Together with bombing raids and nightly blackouts, the food shortages were having a devastating effect on Berliners. Especially frightening was the disappearance of many Jews and other people. The radio announcer that Afra listened to every day was sent to a concentration camp. And who could say what might happen to you if you mentioned his name? Popular movie stars were missing, and it was rumored that the talented actor Hans Otto had thrown himself out of a fourth story window. The master of ceremonies at the Cleopatra Cabaret committed suicide, as did a famous cartoonist.

During this period, exactly as Afra had predicted, transiting Saturn was in exact conjunction to Hitler's Sun and transiting Pluto was squaring his Sun, clearly indicating a time of thwarted ambitions, of gloomy despair.

Chapter 22

Even with the restrictions the Gestapo placed on her, Afra couldn't ignore the sad plight of the Jewish people. She knew Hitler hated the Jews and was convinced they were responsible for everything that was wrong with the world. Most of them had been forced from their homes and were living in secret hiding places or continuously moving about to avoid detection. When they surreptitiously contacted Afra she gave them food stamps and encouragement. Armed with her ephemeris recovered from its safe place she warned them when particularly dangerous times were approaching.

Marthe came to her one evening after dark. The obligatory Star of David was sewn on the sleeve of her worn overcoat. She was trying to hold herself together, but looked ready to break down in tears.

Afra brought out the teapot and cups, and they sat together in her office. With a small, sad sigh, Marthe related her story. "My husband and I were at a meeting and someone made a derogatory remark about the Nazis. Immediately my husband put his finger to his mouth and whispered, 'Shh, shh. Do you see that little hole in the window? Anyone could listen there and report everything we say.'"

Marthe's hand was shaking so badly she set her teacup down. "Somebody must have said something to the Nazis about my husband because he didn't come home the next day. Afra, he hasn't been back in over a week." Her voice had risen in panic, and she cried out, "The Nazis murdered him! I know it, but I don't know why!" Helpless and hopeless, tears streamed down her pale cheeks. In vain, she wiped them with a handkerchief.

Afra's heart cried out to Marthe as she put her hand on her trembling shoulder.

Finally, Marthe pulled herself together, "Afra, it's getting worse. More and more Jewish families are being robbed of their belongings, sent off to concentration camps or shot on the spot. People shout hateful words and throw rocks at my sons as they walk down the street. I don't know what to do."

"While I set up your chart I want you to close your eyes and relax," Afra said. "I'll find out what's the best thing for you to do."

She studied the progressions, while Marthe sipped fortifying tea. After ten minutes of scrutiny Afra said, "I'm afraid you're right, Marthe. Your husband is gone, but I feel he's still here with you in spirit." Marthe squeezed her eyes shut and clamped her hands over her mouth. Afra continued in a positive tone. "You and your sons are going to be just fine. But you must leave Germany. Luckily, you have an astrological doorway. It will be slammed shut in five days. It's a matter of life and death that you go before then. Leave quietly. Don't tell anyone. Don't withdraw a large sum of money from the bank. Things will be hard for a while, but within a year your life and your sons' lives will take a big turn for the better."

Marthe was still hurting, but Afra had given her hope that she and her sons would be all right. Afra showed her to the door where they said their goodbyes. Marthe disappeared into the night.

It was difficult for Afra to comprehend the stupendous evil Hitler was perpetrating on the Jews and other people on his hate list. Scores of people were being picked up by the Gestapo — vanishing into the night and fog.

Thousands of Jews left Germany.

Chapter 23

During the 1930's an Anglo-German "cultural society" in Britain called The Link had been implicated in espionage activities and subsequently dissolved. This incident gave future novelist Ian Fleming of the Department of Naval Intelligence an idea he shared with his chief, Maxwell Knight. "If the Nazis could be made to believe The Link is still in existence, we could use it to bait the Nazi leaders. We could convince the Nazis that The Link has enough influence to overthrow Churchill's government and install one that would readily negotiate a separate peace with Hitler."

"But who among the Nazi leadership is gullible enough to fall for such a story?" asked Maxwell.

"I already thought of that. What about Hitler's Deputy Fuhrer, Rudolph Hess? Unlike all the suspicious and conniving Nazi leaders, Hess is a trusting, not too bright man, who surrounds himself with mystics and astrologers. Anyway, he's something of an Anglophile. Our intelligence sources are aware that he's anxious for peace with England so Germany can concentrate on defeating Russia. In Hess's mind Russia is the real enemy."

"Yes," agreed Maxwell slowly nodding his head, "I agree with you. Rudolf Hess is the obvious choice."

"Now listen to this," said Fleming. "I know a Swiss astrologer who can work up some astrological advice proposing a peace mission to England. This can be passed on to Hess by Dr. Schultze-Strathaus, an astrological adviser on Hess's staff. Furthermore, I'm sure we can persuade the Duke of Hamilton, who has access to Churchill and the King, to receive a visit from Hess for that purpose."

The two men were well satisfied with the plan.

The Swiss astrologer chose May 10, 1941 as the appropriate date. An unusual conjunction of six planets in Taurus would take place at that time.

Dr. Schultze-Strathaus called for a meeting with Hess. He explained, "This planetary lineup will be an auspicious time for a mission of global ramifications." He explained in a confidential tone, "You must secretly fly to Great Britain. You will meet the Duke of Hamilton to discuss a peace treaty between England and Germany. Then we will have free rein against the Soviet Union."

To cinch it all off, a close friend told Hess of a dream in which Hess flew a plane to an important destination. In a second dream, Hess was in a magnificent castle, walking through halls lined with tartan-tapestries.

Hess hated the idea of doing something without Hitler's knowledge. However, he was no longer Deputy Fuhrer, and had gradually fallen into the background. If he succeeded in this grand peacemaking mission perhaps he could recapture the favor of the leader he worshipped.

Hess, an experienced pilot, independently commandeered a ME-110 fighter plane. Upon reaching England he sighted a railway south of the Duke's residence. When he saw the speed gauge indicate zero he switched off the motor to parachute down. Opening the hatch, he faced a streaming rush of air and hurriedly flung himself out of the plane. He pulled at the parachute ring, and his parachute flew open. As he descended the plane crashed in a nearby field. A farmer witnessed the whole scene and marched him off to the Home Guard.

Hess told the English authorities about the amazing astrological prediction. Instead of an enthusiastic reception as peacemaker and hero, he was thrown into prison, treated as a lowly prisoner of war.

The minute the news got out it caused all kinds of political trouble. Hitler didn't want Russia or Italy to get the idea he was making a separate peace with England. All would be lost if Hess revealed Hitler's secret plan to invade Russia.

He immediately called an emergency convocation of Gauleiters and Reichsleiters. "Hess's flight was sheer insanity," he said angrily. "He's a deserter. If I catch him he will pay as an ordinary traitor." He ranted on, "I'm sure he was influenced by astrologers. They brainwashed him into committing this treacherous act. It's time to put an end to those stargazers."

There were rumors that many astrologers had already predicted a doomed future for Hitler and the Reich. This bad propaganda had to be stopped.

The Gestapo arrested and questioned hundreds of astrologers, gypsies and occult practitioners not sanctioned by the Nazi Party. Some, including Schultze-Strathaus, were sent to the camps. Others were singled out for elimination and never seen again. The Gestapo also confiscated astrological books, papers and other forbidden literature. Fortunately, Afra had taken the precaution of putting her clients' charts, astrology books and notes in a bank box. She cancelled her few appointments indefinitely. Nobody was safe.

When she read news reports implying Hess had a history of mental problems, she wondered why Hitler had retained him so long in high office.

Chapter 24

Fists pounded on the front door abruptly awaking Afra. She sat up, alert. The nightstand clock pointed to 5:30 AM. She knew it could only be the Gestapo, a frightening thought because her horoscope indicated 8 AM to 11 AM that day would be a dangerous time. What if someone had spoken against her? Would she be sent to a concentration camp? She threw on her robe. A stream of possibilities, all bad, raced through her head.

Hurrying to the front door, she cautiously opened it a few inches. Before her two officers wearing Gestapo black leather coats and black hats stood stiffly. One was small-boned and short; the other had the pudgy, greasy face of a sausage lover atop bulky shoulders.

"Frau Waesch?"

She nodded, tightening the cord of her robe.

"Get dressed," the big one ordered. "We're taking you to the police station." He slapped his boot with a rubber stick.

Blood drained from her face. Like all the Gestapo, these men were hard, arrogant and contemptuous, ready to kill Germans or foreigners.

"Wait here," Afra said, "I'll get dressed and tell my daughter that I'm going with you." She hastened to her bedroom and shut the door. What could she wear? Like everyone else in Germany her clothes were old and shabby; her shoes scruffy. Her navy blue dress with yellow trim would have to do.

Lilo tapped on the door. "What's going on, Mutti?"

"Now don't worry, Lilo." She struggled to keep her voice from shaking. "Those officers are taking me to the police station. It's probably some routine thing." She clutched her purse to stop her trembling hands. It was a good thing Ellen was off with Yvonne performing for the soldiers.

The minute Afra opened the front door the Gestapo men grasped her elbows. They hustled her out of the building to a dark vehicle. Frightened out of her wits, she thought, they killed Willi. They could kill me!

Astrologers, palm readers, occultists and healers were crammed into the police station. The din of sobbing and frightened voices filled the atmosphere. It was dreadfully ominous.

Afra struggled to summon up her courage. Several coarse looking Gestapo officers strode through the crowd keeping order. After a while, an officer emerged from a doorway. His clean-cut, intelligent appearance set him apart. Perhaps he could help her. Edging over, she struck up a conversation. "How do you do, sir? My name is Frau Waesch. Could I could ask you a question?"

"Certainly, Frau Waesch." He turned to her with a small bow. "Please come in my office. It's quieter."

Her innate courage returned. She followed him in and he closed the door. "Do you know how long I'll be kept here?"

"I'm sorry, I have no idea. I'm a member of the local police force. When the Gestapo is involved I must follow their orders."

Her quest for immediate release was quashed. She slowly inhaled, realizing she'd scarcely breathed since she heard the pounding on her apartment door. She glanced through the window. The last of the detainees were being herded into a van. "What's happening?" she asked anxiously.

"They're going to Gestapo Headquarters at Alexanderplatz. It appears you've been overlooked." They walked into the empty room. "I'll send you by subway with one of my officers."

Afra's stomach twisted. Gestapo Headquarters was the most feared place in Berlin. In its confines hundreds, maybe thousands, of people had been interrogated and tortured. They simply disappeared. The other people arrested with her were on their way there. She peeked at her watch. It was exactly 10 AM. One hour to go. She said to the policeman, "I'm so nervous I must try to pull myself together. Would it be possible to wait until 11 o'clock to hand me over?"

"I suppose so," he said reluctantly. He led her over to a chair beside a large cell fronted with iron bars. It was full of people. Half of the detainees were sitting hunched over or lying on the floor. The rest were milling about, eyes haunted and empty, movements stiff and mechanical. A constant agitation of moans, crying and hysterical laughter gnawed on Afra's nerves. Smells of mold, sweat, feces and urine permeated the air.

"Who are those people?" Afra asked the policeman, trying to keep her voice composed.

He spoke indifferently, "Hitler ordered the Gestapo to send all insane people and mental defectives to the camps. There's no room for them in the hospitals." He gave her a nod. "Wait here, Frau Waesch," he said and walked away.

She sat tentatively. Nervously she looked in the cell. The people did appear crazy. One detainee came close to her. He didn't seem to be dangerous and was behind bars, but she automatically moved her chair a few inches away. There was something repellant about him.

He grasped the bars showing white knuckles. He leaned toward her. The large dark pits of his sunken eyes fixed upon her in wild fear. "Where am I?" he frantically whispered.

"The police station," Afra briefly replied. She didn't want to attract attention, but she did turn her chair toward the caged man.

"Strang is my name," he said, spraying spit. He began a rambling tirade about his situation and the terrible conditions. Interspersed with a stream of pointless words he asked repeatedly, "Can you help get me out of here?"

"I'm afraid not, Herr Strang. "I'm a detainee. I'd like nothing better than to be somewhere else."

He stared right through her.

Afra felt compassion and anguish for Strang. Might she get into trouble talking to him? Thankfully, he walked away muttering to himself. But in his unhinged state he kept stealing meaningless glances back to see if she was still there. Each time, she lowered her eyes, not wanting to encourage him. By tomorrow they'd all probably be in a concentration camp -- or an even more dreadful fate.

She checked her watch. Forty minutes to go before the difficult constellation will have moved. Waiting, she gave way to fright. Hitler's oppressive regime had closed in on everyone, like a tightening vise. If she were lucky enough to get out of the Gestapo alive, she was going to have to make some major life changes to survive those difficult times.

"Please come with me, Frau Waesch." It was the same policeman. He drove her to Gestapo Headquarters and left her in a cramped and cluttered office. A clerk typed her answers to his questions. Fifteen minutes later, he brought her to an interrogation room at Gestapo Headquarters. Two men stiffly sat behind a table, a Gestapo officer and a civilian wearing a suit.

"Sit down, Frau Waesch," said the officer, an ugly man with a permanent scowl etched on his face. Papers rustled while he and his cohort whispered over her documentation. It was maddening. Minutes dragged by. Finally the officer looked up. He gave a quick nod to his companion.

He informed Afra, "Herr Visser, an astrologer with the Nazi Occult Bureau, has reported you are practicing astrology."

"Sir," she said, "I only help people with their problems. I've never been in trouble." She strove to keep her voice conciliatory.

"I'm not a wandering gypsy. I live in a nice apartment near Kurfurstendamm. My daughter works for the Special Services."

Bored, the official said, "Herr Visser will interview you."

Afra turned her edgy attention to Visser. He seemed lifeless. Perhaps it was his lank hair, colorless face, and downward curved lips. Only his eyes were alive. They burned malevolence.

A shudder passed through her. Psychically she knew he was a man to be feared.

Visser began reading questions from a sheet of paper. "Have you ever had Hitler's horoscope in your possession?"

"Of course, Herr Visser. In the past every newspaper kiosk had publications with his chart."

"And what is Hitler's horoscope like?" he asked, spiteful curiosity lurking in his pale eyes.

"Oh, very interesting, very unusual," she took care not to indicate whether good or bad.

Visser gave her a look of disgust. Once more he consulted his paper. "Should members of different races – Aryans, Jews, Chinese and Negroes – born at the same place under identical constellations expect the same astrological interpretations?"

If Afra admitted race wasn't a consideration in horoscopes, she would deny Aryan superiority. She wasn't going to be tricked into trouble by that question. Somehow she managed to contrive an evasive answer. He let it pass and she felt a welcome release of tension.

After a series of questions, he and the Gestapo official huddled together. She could hardly breathe. Her life was hanging on their decision. The phone on the table rang. The head official picked it up. "*Guten morgen*, Captain Roth speaking." He listened intently and said, "Certainly, Reichfuhrer Himmler, we will take care of it immediately." With an angry frown he put the receiver down.

He turned to Afra. "Frau Waesch, you will be free to go after you sign a declaration that you will not mention your arrest to anyone, contact any of your former clients, or in the future practice astrology in any shape or form, or even to refer to it in conversation. Let me warn you, Fraulein Waesch. Incarceration in a concentration camp will be immediate at the slightest infringement of these instructions." He leaned toward her. His fierce eyes drilled into her.

Herr Visser was seething furiously.

Afra noted it was exactly 11 AM.

Her home! Her door! She turned the key in the lock. Lilo jumped off the sofa the minute she came in. "Mutti," she cried, "I'm so glad you're back! I called Himmler's office and left a message about your arrest."

"Thank goodness!" exclaimed Afra.

"Mutti, there's also bad news. Soon after you left one of those awful Gestapo men came back. They emptied your office. It's outrageous that these people can walk in and loot." Lilo's eyes flashed with righteous anger.

Afra rushed to her office. The few innocuous books she'd saved were gone, papers littered everywhere. "What a mess!" she exclaimed. But she was relieved to find nothing of importance missing, and said to Lilo, "Fortunately I safely hid my clients' confidential charts, ephemeris and astrology books." She stood amidst the disarray. Dazed. She didn't know where to start cleaning up.

Lilo, as usual, took over. "Have you had lunch yet, Mutti?" she asked. Afra shook her head, and Lilo led her out of the room. "Come with me. I made you some hot soup." They went to the kitchen and Afra gratefully sat down while Lilo made toast and warmed up the soup.

"Lilo, I'm thankful I'm home." By following the planets' warning she'd avoided a concentration camp — or worse, a firing squad.

Nevertheless, she was worried about Visser, and called Egon. She told him about being taken off to the Gestapo and asked, "What do you know about a man named Visser with the Nazi Occult Bureau?"

"Jeorg Visser is one of the worst Nazis. He's an enigmatic and powerful figure in the Bureau. Of course, the Bureau, like every other facet of Hitler's regime, is riddled with rivalries to curry Hitler's favor." Egon's voice took on an ominous tone. "I don't want to frighten you Afra, but Visser is ruthlessly ambitious and morbidly jealous of competition. Should he perceive you were encroaching on his domain, he would be vindictive. Even violent. This is a man you want to stay clear of."

"I will," she said, promising herself to be absolutely cautious. That Nazi's eyes had borne down on her fearsomely. She was sure he wouldn't forget her. She'd watch every word that came out of her mouth. Take no chances.

Chapter 25

Just as Hitler was ready to invade Russia, Visser and his team of astrologers advised him to avoid taking risky chances or the treasury money would be quickly depleted. His generals also offered warnings.

What fools! What did they know? Although he was tormented about the possibility of his great plans failing, nothing would stop him. He was going to conquer that country of unbounded land and wealth.

He paced back and forth in his office until a wave of fatigue forced him to sit down. With his elbows on his knees, his hands pressed to his temples, he rocked in despair. He lay on the sofa, closed his eyes to shut out the world, but sleep eluded him.

He imagined himself inside his Chamber of Stars. It had always been a pleasant daydream to be in his private planetarium, gazing up at the stars, planets and constellations as they moved through the heavens. That day it seemed to his troubled mind that the heavenly bodies were spinning out of control. He feared he was going insane.

He remembered Afra Waesch, the astrologer who had annoyed him when he took her to Eagle's Nest. Still, Himmler never let him forget how she had saved his life by picking a successful day for his operation. He rang his secretary. "Please have Frau Afra Waesch brought to me immediately. With her ephemeris."

Afra barely had time to change, brush her hair, and grab her charts and ephemeris before Hitler's chauffeur appeared at the door. As they hurried towards the car she caught a brief glimpse of a familiar pigeon through a flurry of snowflakes. Fifteen minutes later they arrived at the Chancellery. When she stepped out of the car, everything was obscured from her view by the block long pink marble building.

At the motor entrance, a black uniformed guard stood arrow straight. The SS silver double-lightning flash insignia and death's head marked his cap. He led her through the courtyard to the grand entrance set behind forty-two foot high columns. He opened the door, and they entered the building, followed by a pigeon flying high above. Oblivious, the guard turned on his well-polished heel and escorted her through one enormous hall after another. Pink mosaic marble floors, thirty-foot ceilings, and large mahogany doors topped with sculpted eagles or emblems were viewed by Afra as just more of Hitler's excesses at a time when Germany's resources were strained by a war nobody wanted.

The long walk led them to an inner chamber where the guard announced Afra to a secretary seated at a desk.

"Good day, Frau Waesch," she said, directing her to one of the chairs lining the wall.

Afra sat, grateful for the time to review Hitler's horoscope. She couldn't help worrying. How could she soften the bleak forecast that lay ahead of him? It wasn't going to be an easy consultation.

Above the oversized door to Hitler's private office was a sculpted plaque of Plato's four Virtues: Wisdom, Fortitude, Temperance and Justice. Inspiring words, but how incongruous, she mused. Hitler had none of those virtues. As it applied to him the plaque should have read foolishness, sneakiness, excessiveness and injustice. His plan to dominate Europe was foolhardy. His motives were underhanded, his temper tantrums childish, and his political assassinations, invasions and corruption unjust.

The door to Hitler's office opened. A shadowy figure stepped out. It was Herr Visser, coming from a disturbing consultation. Nothing pleased the Fuhrer those days, he thought. No matter how much he searched through his astrological charts he couldn't find any positive prognostications to mitigate the negative indicators pointing to more delays and obstacles in the war. Instead of heeding the signs, Hitler verbally attacked him.

Now here was that quack astrologer Afra Waesch again. Sitting there like she owned the place. She had already dazzled Himmler by a lucky guess when she picked a good day for his surgery. Now she was fooling around with Hitler's head. Who knew what she'd come up with next? It grated him no end that Hitler would consider calling in a stupid woman when he'd already given his own superior expertise. His mouth turned hard and cruel. He stared at her long and hatefully as he slowly crossed the room.

Afra got his message, surrounded herself with God's protection. As he turned away, she knew he was shaken by her poise. She was only too glad to see him go. His unpleasant and sinister vibrations left with him.

Minutes later, the phone rang. "Yes, my Fuhrer," the secretary answered. She ushered Afra into his office.

Hitler was standing at the far end of a spacious room beside a magnificent desk. He was wearing black trousers and a gray double-breasted jacket. On his sleeve was the same eagle emblem carved above the doors along the corridor. At first she thought he'd shrunk in stature. No longer the powerful speaker idolized by captivated audiences, he'd become a tired, stoop-shouldered old man dwarfed by an enormous room with extra-large doors, windows and furniture.

Afra's walk toward his oppressive presence seemed to take forever. "Heil Hitler," she said, reluctantly lifting her arm.

Halfheartedly he raised his hand. It humiliated and irritated him to consult a lowly female astrologer. Still, he reminded himself, she'd been highly recommended by Himmler whose judgment he trusted. She'd surely find a positive planetary configuration that would help him achieve his goals, unlike Visser and his other astrologers who were consistently failing him.

Afra noted the fatigue in his face, the fear in his eyes. He appeared to be on the verge of a breakdown. Then, unexpectedly, her intuition revealed he was trapped by horrific memories of his father's brutal beatings. He had vowed to would never again be controlled. Whatever it took, whomever he hurt, he would always maintain total power.

He stared at her with faded but still hypnotic eyes to establish his authority. Noticing her composure and strength, he thought perhaps she might have something positive to offer.

Afra felt no contact with him as was her intention. She avoided staring into his eyes knowing he'd feel threatened. To survive the encounter, she knew she would have to skirt issues. Under no circumstances could she suggest he was losing the war. Her plan was to say as little as possible and get out quickly.

He awkwardly waved his hand toward an upholstered chair. "Please sit down Frau Waesch." He sat behind his desk.

He said casually, as if the matter was minor, "I'd like you to look at my horoscope. Perhaps you have some suggestions as to what direction is fortunate. I will leave you for a half hour to set up your charts." With that, he handed her his birth information and left the room. His maniacal eyes reminded her of the gravity of her situation.

She already had his completed horoscope, progressions and transits in her folder. The astrological indications clearly showed his lucky streak was at an end; his future was taking a sharp turn for the worse. It was equally certain his Taurean bullheadedness wouldn't allow him to change course. She needed to be very careful not to arouse his wrath.

When he returned, she gathered her charts together and commented as tactfully as she could, "Right now, my Fuhrer, your progressed Moon is in Scorpio. Transiting Pluto is retrograde and squares your Sun. Although you feel compelled to force your goals through against all opposition, this is a time to slow down and reevaluate. This period calls for self-control and cooperation. Powerful forces are arrayed against you. The scene is shifting. Right now it's impossible to keep the power in your own hands."

Her words struck him like a knife plunging into his heart. He struggled to control himself.

Afra felt the immensity of his fury by the flame in his eyes and the rigid muscles of his neck. She gripped the arms of her chair. Though she didn't mention it, the Pluto transit also indicated that not only was he surrounded by outer conditions of breakdown and decay, but he was obviously also suffering from a physical and mental breakdown. Instead, she said, "With transiting Saturn conjunct to your Sun, the additional responsibility of taking on a new project would be too much."

She lowered her eyes to her notes. "Herr Hitler, right now you are experiencing major financial burdens and shortages. It behooves you to hold back and curtail your objectives." Cautiously, she looked up. "My Fuhrer, if you spread yourself too thin, an overwhelming financial crisis will ensue."

"Frau Waesch," he spit out with barely controlled rage, "you have absolutely no idea what I must do to accomplish Germany's great destiny. I alone can do this!"

Afra was compelled to speak up. "But my Fuhrer, the whole point of astrology is to take advantage of the planetary forces, to march ahead when the planets are favorable, and to pause and wait when the planets are inharmoniously positioned."

"Stop!" he screamed, jumping up and waving his good arm hysterically. His eyes blazed with fury. Blood hammered in his temples. "I should have known better then to consult a fool woman! Don't you realize you're in the presence of the greatest German who ever lived?" He launched into a rant of how much he'd done and how he'd established Germany as a major force throughout Europe. He recited in lengthy detail his diplomatic tactics and numerous conquests.

Afra stared at him speechless. The words of St. Mathew were imprinted in glowing letters before her mind, "Whosoever will be great among you, let him be your minister." She knew the word minister referred to someone who reached out to serve others. True greatness came from service motivated by love.

"I've heard enough!" Hitler's harsh voice broke over her. He thought to himself, I'll kill that damn woman! He stalked around his desk and stood before her. His eyes were hard as granite, his face blotchy and purple. Then, just as he clenched his right hand in a fist, a car honked outside. In that instant he was back in reality. What would people say if he killed someone in his glorious pink Chancellery? In a hate-filled voice he said, "That will be all, Frau Waesch."

Afra was certain he was crazy. In truth, he had only called her in for a verification of his megalomania. His dictatorship was based on only one goal, an ongoing extension of his power, no matter whom or what he destroyed. Without a word or a backward glance, she picked up her papers and hurried toward the door.

Once more Hitler's demonic rage was about to take over. Suddenly and seeming from nowhere, he began to see a vision.

Appearing before him was a host of angels led by a male angel ablaze with light. His white hair fell in waves to his shoulders. His blue eyes were full of sorrow and resolve. Pasch pointed his finger. "You must go!" he commanded the demon inside Hitler.

A force, akin to lightening, thrust Hitler to the floor.

The demon jeeringly hissed as he fled, "I'll return when you're asleep" he whispered to Hitler.

In a blink Pasch was gone. Hitler lay sprawled on the carpet, gripped in terror.

Afra, unaware of Pasch's timely rescue, saw none of this as she exited the room. The whole encounter with Hitler had left her numb. He was so rigidly set in his opinions that he was incapable of rational judgment. There was no hope for Germany as long as he was in power. She shuddered to think what he'd have done if she'd told him his horoscope showed defeat in April 1945.

A SS guard escorted her back through the endless corridors. The heels of his shoes rapped against the marble floor, filling her with mounting fear. She dreaded to think of what lay ahead. Would the Gestapo be waiting for her? Suppose she made it home, there was no telling when they'd come hammering on her door.

As she walked out of the building her friend, the pigeon, flew past her up into a shaft of sunlight.

Hitler felt glued to the carpet. The terrifying Angel had rendered him weak and helpless. With a mighty effort he focused his will power, barely managing to crawl to his desk. He lifted himself into his chair and mumbled, "I'll call Himmler and have that dumkopf astrologer shot." He reached for the telephone but suddenly fell back in his chair when he remembered the angel's pointed finger. Slumping forward on his desk, he closed his eyes against a world of dark despair.

Chapter 26

Despite the gloomy atmosphere pervading Berlin, Lilo was radiantly happy and passionately in love with Richard Huebner. He had recently received a sizeable inheritance from his aunt that included a big apartment. The first time he took Lilo there, he unlocked the front door, swept her off her feet and carried her into the lavish living room. They stood on a plush carpet, kissing madly, oblivious to their surroundings. He held her slim waist in his hands, moved up to her rib cage, felt her shiver and draw closer. He ran his hand down her spine. She pushed her hips against him. She struggled with the knot of his tie. He yanked it off, tossed it over his shoulder. He led her across the room, drew her onto the sofa. Bending down, he kissed her knees, her thighs, each touch of his lips melding them closer. He struggled out of his clothes, watching her unbutton her dress until it dropped open. He kissed her breasts, her stomach. She pulled him to her, brought her knees up, urging him on.

Afra knew Lilo had plenty of admirers. But Lilo had never been so taken with anyone as she was with Richard. She talked about him all the time. "Mutti," she said, "he truly loves me, and he cares about the world around him, too. He wants the best for Germany."

Oh yes, Afra thought. She liked Richard. Although she totally disagreed with his enthusiasm for Hitler, she respected his idealism. Along with many others, he was caught up in Hitler's spell. He believed he was following a vision of Germany as it should be.

Their courtship was short. Richard said to Lilo, "Now that I've been drafted into the army and England has declared war on us I think we should get married right away. Our future is so uncertain I want us to be together as much as possible while we can."

"Oh yes, my darling!" cried Lilo nestling her head on his chest. "Nothing could ever make me happier."

"First I'm required to get permission to marry from the military. The Nazi regime only sanctions marriages between healthy people and with both families having pure Aryan ancestry dating back over 250 years."

"Well then, everything's all right," sighed Lilo.

They decided because of the war they'd have a simple wedding with only Afra, Ellen, Yvonne, Richard's parents and a few friends attending. The Justice of the Peace, wearing the brown uniform of the SA, led the wedding party to his office. It was a small room, drab but neat and tidy. Lilo and Richard exuded waves of happiness. Lilo wore a long white gown and the pearl earrings Afra had given her. In her hands was a bouquet of white roses and delicately trailing ferns. She looked at Richard, her heart brimming with love – surely he was the most perfect, lovable and handsome man she had ever known in her short life.

The marriage took place beneath a very large portrait of Adolph Hitler at his villa in the Bavarian countryside. The Fuhrer stood with his back straight, his soldier's cape theatrically draped over his shoulders. His right hand rested on the head of a noble

German Shepherd. The Justice of the Peace concluded the brief ceremony stating, "In the name of the Reich, I declare you henceforth and forever husband and wife." The couple drew together and kissed, absorbed in each other.

Afra's eyes were drawn to the portrait of Hitler. It looked as though his strange eyes were targeted directly on Richard, holding him firmly in his grasp. A chill ran through her body – a fear of Hitler's power over Richard's life and the lives of so many others.

Lilo moved into his beautiful apartment. There they rejoiced in their brief time together. She became pregnant just before he left for Langwasser Camp on his assignment as a tank gunner. Following intense training, he was sent on a tour of duty to France after it capitulated. However, he missed Lilo and longed to be fighting for his Fuhrer and the Nazi principles he believed in.

~~

"Do not tell me what I should do!" Demon-driven Hitler shouted when his generals and astrologers said it would be a fatal mistake to take on a two front war. He knew it was going to be a huge and dangerous undertaking, but he was resolute. He also had a fear that Stalin, Russia's arrogant dictator, might decide to add Germany to his vast empire.

"I, and only I, am in command!" he declared to his generals. "Everyone must obey me without question."

~~

Following a two-week leave, Richard was transferred to the Russian Front for Operation Barbarrosa, the massive invasion of Russia. He wrote to Lilo, *I'm with the 7th Panzer Division. We're a well-trained fighting unit, ready to fight to the end and be victorious. Please don't worry; the Soviet Union is a sluggish giant.*

Back in Berlin Lilo heard the sharp sounds of marching boots outside the apartment. Platoons of SA storm troopers and SS men were constantly making their way through the streets. Tanks followed behind them, rattling the windowpanes.

June 22, 1941 – German cannon flashed and roared along a thousand mile line from the icy Arctic Circle to the warm Black Sea. Richard, together with three million German soldiers, drove deep into the Soviet Union with an overwhelming blitzkrieg attack. They were the greatest tank force ever concentrated on one front, equipped with nearly 10,000 tanks and supplemented with marching columns of infantry. 3,000 German planes crossed the borders and bombed Soviet airfields, smashing aircraft on the ground by the hundreds. German forces made their way into Vilna, Lithuania and then turned toward Minsk in Russia proper.

Lilo read the newspapers and listened to the radio, avidly following the progress of the Wehrmacht. Day after day she waited for the mail with mixed feelings. It could, after all, be news of Richard's death.

July 6, 1941 – *My one and only Sweetheart, how I miss you. I have your picture taped on the control panel in our tank.*

I'm sending you a picture of me and my tank buddy Brandt Wilhelm. You can see we're dusty and grimy and tanned by the sun. Brandt says to tell you hello.

We're only fighting against fragmented opposition. Russia is nothing but poverty and heart breaking misfortune.

Three days later, the Germans overran twenty-one Soviet rifle divisions and fourteen tank brigades, took 300,000 prisoners and destroyed 2,600 tanks and some 1,500 guns of the Red Army. In his next letter, Richard was confident. *Brandt and I and the rest of the guys believe the war will be over this year. We trust the Fuhrer completely.*

While all the military victories were going on, Lilo gave birth to a baby boy. She fell in love with the child, even before he was born. He was the most incredible thing that ever happened to her. He looked just like Richard with the same curly brown hair and expressive eyes that watched her every moment with undeviating love. It was like having a part of Richard with her. She named him Richard, nicknamed Ricky.

~~

December 11, 1941 – Hitler was on a roll. He declared war against the United States. "Don't bother me with unimportant considerations," he told his staff. "The U.S. is just another decadent bourgeois democracy with a mixture of races and a lack of discipline. Look how easy it was for the Japanese to attack Pearl Harbor."

~~

Lilo was elated when she heard the Wehrmacht broadcaster announce that Soviet resistance in Stalingrad had been wiped out. She was sure Hitler's power was greater and more firmly established than ever before. But Afra was still worried. With millions of men off fighting, Germany's resources – both human and material – were being stretched to the limit. Old men, adolescents and women were needed to fuel the gigantic war machine.

Inevitably, Lilo was conscripted to work at a munitions factory and worked twelve hours a day six days a week. With such a grueling schedule she was grateful Mutti had moved in with her.

Afra adored Ricky. It was a joy to be with him in an otherwise troubled world. He was a bright boy and exceptionally curious. He investigated everything he saw, and as soon as he learned to talk he began asking questions. He loved to listen to Afra read him bedtime stories.

The fall weather became cool. The leaves on the trees turned yellow and orange and finally dropped, lying in brown clusters on the ground. The outdoor cafes moved indoors, leaving chairs and tables stacked under awnings. Berlin became a winter city with gray skies and cold winds. When Afra, Lilo and Ricky went out they bundled up in warm clothes. Lilo worried Richard would be caught in the onslaught of the frigid Russian winter.

At last a letter arrived. *The stupid Russians thought we'd back off from the oncoming winter. We're certain that once this battle is over, peace will reign for Germany and all Europe. My dearest Lilo, I love you forever.*

~~

Unfortunately, Hitler had a tendency to alternate between aggression and procrastination. It was as though two totally different personalities vacillated back and forth. This time he delayed too long, and almost overnight Richard's division was caught in the fury of the Russian winter. The temperature dropped to 40 degrees below zero. Hitler, having anticipated a swift victory, had refused to issue adequate clothing and food supplies. Thousands were half starved, tormented by frostbite or freezing to death. Oil congealed in motors, automatic weapons froze, artillery failed to function. The inaction along with perpetual bad weather and hunger sapped the spirits of the soldiers. They desperately waited for orders, 13,000 miles away from Germany.

January 10, 1943 -- Richard read over his last letter to Lilo. *When we first invaded Russia, I was sure we were invincible. But dearest Lilo, now the Russians are rallying with a vengeance. But most terrible is that my friend Brandt's leg and knee were badly wounded. He's being sent back to a hospital in Berlin not far from you, and it looks like he will be out of the war. Maybe you could look in on him.*

I never thought I would ever be so far away from you, but I love you as much as ever. I hope this letter slips past the censors.

Lilo's eyes filled with tears. She thought about the wasted years, with Richard so far away in a doomed war.

In spite of their heavy losses, the Russians rallied a resistance such as the Wehrmacht had never encountered. There were more of them and they had better equipment than Hitler had ever dreamed possible. Finally the Sixth Army was completely surrounded. General Paulus, in a desperate attempt to save the lives of his remaining troops, radioed a message to Hitler explaining it was futile for the Sixth Army to fight on.

Hitler, obsessed with fear of failure, ordered, "Surrender is forbidden. The Sixth Army will hold their position to the last man and the last round. By their heroic endurance they will make an unforgettable contribution toward the establishment of a defensive front and the salvation of the Western world."

January 31, 1943 — Completely surrounded, Paulus surrendered the battered, sick and dying remnants of his army to the Russians. Richard along with 91,000 other German prisoners began a forced march to labor camps in faraway Siberia. The land stretched out silently before them. Gray clouds streamed across the sky. Bare trees swayed in biting wind bearing down from the north. Wolves howled in the distance. Richard plodded along a seemingly endless march, struggling to put one foot in front of the other. His face, feet and hands were numb with cold. He dropped everything he was carrying except a bit of food. He and many of his fellow soldiers kept falling behind.

Despite his suffering, his heart was filled with tender love for Lilo and the son he didn't even know. What's happening to me? Richard wondered. I've hardly lived and yet I'm going farther and farther away from those I love, my home and my country. I've scarcely had any time with Lilo. I've never even seen my son.

A cold front surrounded them with snow that turned into icy pellets. The miles dragged on. Bone weary, he sank into a snow bank. He drifted into a comforting darkness, no longer hungry, no longer cold. He dreamed of Lilo and Ricky. Relentlessly the wind blew snow over him and the endless white land.

~~

The strains of defeat were taking a toll on Hitler's health. Every morning professor Morell, his personal physician, gave him so-called vitamin injections that actually were amphetamine. Immediately the drug made him more alert. But long term use of the drug damaged his nervous system causing aggressive, manic states followed by mental exhaustion and fatigue. Eventually, the habitual use of amphetamine caused advanced mental dysfunction, including poor judgment. Hitler became increasingly irrational and reckless sending tens of thousands of soldiers to Russia to die.

Chapter 27

The defeat at Stalingrad and the annihilation of the Afrika Korps shook the Germans' faith in Hitler. For the first time, the people were aware that Germany could lose the war.

Berliners were dominated by never ending wartime demands. Everyone was hungry, scores of people were sick, and many of the very young and the very old died of starvation. Shoes were worn out. Clothes were in short supply. Water was restricted to one bath a week. Afra could feel the dust and dirt clinging to her from the bombing raids. Wounded soldiers shuffled around in the streets, staring into space or looking for stray cigarette butts on the sidewalks.

Lilo checked the newspaper every day, running her fingers with dread down the lists of the dead. She had not received mail for two months and feared the worst. Bombing by Britain, the United States, France and Russia were incessant. Suddenly her thoughts were cut short by the familiar sound of a siren that meant another air raid was on its way.

Afra, Lilo and Ricky ran to the dreary basement shelter. Overhead they heard the pounding of anti-aircraft guns, the drone of enemy planes, the dull thudding of a nearby hit. The shelter had a dank smell. In a few places Afra noticed water seeping down the walls. A lone light bulb hung from the ceiling. Upright tree trunks served as extra support beams. Over thirty people were people crowded in the basement. Afra and her family huddled in a corner with blankets to keep warm. They listened to the radio to while the time away, though the music was all but drowned out by the bombing.

A woman mending a shirt by the light of a kerosene lamp looked up and said in a peevish voice, "What I don't understand is how all this came about when in the beginning Hitler did so many wonderful things for us?" A nearby bomb exploded and the ground trembled. She ducked and covered her head with her hands.

Afra kept her thoughts to herself. Defeatist remarks were verboten and one could end up in a concentration camp for incriminating comments. She knew Hitler had never really done anything for the people. Everything he did was for himself. He brainwashed the people and programmed the children into supporting him.

"This is just a temporary set back," said a man sitting by himself in the murky shadows. "The Fuhrer says it's certain Germany will win the war."

His optimistic statement was followed by the booming of shells. The ground shook. One of the supporting tree trunks toppled over barely missing a young woman and her baby. Afra looked up, fearful that the house had been struck and would collapse on them. Although the light bulb was swaying back and forth, everything remained in place. The din of the bombing receded. They all left the cellar. Just outside the door was a bomb crater, the size of a small pond.

December 24, 1943 — For a change, the day began on a happier note. "Welcome, welcome!" Afra, Lilo and Ricky cried in chorus as Ellen and Yvonne burst in the front door of Lilo's apartment. Their arms were full of suitcases and packages.

"Put everything down," Afra said as she gave them big hugs, "and take a seat."

"It's good to be back," said Ellen, glancing around the living room. A small artificial Christmas tree with glittering ornaments stood in the corner — out of place with the shabby furniture and threadbare carpet. She flopped down on the faded sofa.

"I'll agree with that," added Yvonne, sitting next to Ellen and stretching her legs out before her.

"How was your tour?" asked Lilo.

"The military treated us very well," answered Yvonne. "Still it was exhausting. A good deal of the time we were in trucks weaving our way around muddy pot holes, burned out tanks, or piles of stones from bombed buildings. It was frightfully cold." She shivered and pulled her jacket tighter around her. "Actually, it's cold here, too."

"We have no fuel," Afra remarked. "People are even chopping down the trees in the Tiergarten." The family's initial happy outburst disintegrated into a cloud of dismal thoughts.

"Cheer up, everyone," chirped Ellen. "Let's not forget this is Christmas Eve."

Lilo," Afra asked, "Would you help me get some of crackers and that ersatz coffee?" They left the room, and Ellen and Yvonne sank back on the sofa, glad to be back and doing nothing.

When everyone warmed up a bit with coffee and momentarily staved off their hunger with a few crackers, Ellen and Yvonne brought out their packages. "Look Ricky," Ellen said, "I think this one is for you."

He jumped up and down and cried out, "Me, me, me!"

Ellen cut the cord and opened the package. "It's a fuzzy teddy bear just for you." He grabbed the bear and raced around the room with it.

Lilo gently interrupted him. "Ricky, don't forget to thank Aunt Ellen."

He ran around the room once more and then went to Ellen. "Thank you, Aunt Ellen." His eyes were full of delight.

Ellen also brought Lilo some perfume, and a sweater for Afra that she had knitted with some yarn someone had given her. Yvonne was only there for a while because she was staying with her mother. She brought some chocolate, a rare treat. Afra was happy to have all of her family with her again. It was almost like Christmas used to be before Hitler took over.

That night they had potatoes, the wartime staple for all German citizens. Afra managed to dress them up a bit with sweet and sour gravy, and they had kriegsbrot, the hard, dark war bread, and tiny helpings of salt herring and turnips.

"I bet," said Lilo, "they gave you better food on your tour."

"It certainly wasn't great, Lilo. But the military has to be sure everyone is well fed. We did have meat and some vegetables besides the potatoes."

Lilo remarked, "It's been years since we've had anything but potatoes. We've had boiled potatoes with white gravy, potatoes boiled in their jackets and peeled at the table, potatoes fried in margarine or lard, and mashed potatoes." She pushed her plate away. "Remember, Mutti, that delicious Schnitzel you used to cook?" Her mouth watered when she thought of the ham roasted with a crisp crackling of skin. The sound of a siren interrupted her reminiscing.

January, 1944 — Afra and her fellow Berliners had been subjected to twenty-four major air raids and hundreds of smaller raids that devastated Berlin and killed or maimed tens of thousands. Anyone with enough strength fought the fires to save what was left from the bombings. They dug through the wreckage looking for loved ones and lost possessions, eyes bleak with despair, shoulders hunched in defeat. Some mornings they had to stay indoors because Russian prisoners were defusing or exploding bombs that hadn't detonated when they'd dropped during the night. The poor men went about their business in silent resignation, knowing at any moment their lives could be over.

In spite of everything, Propaganda Minister Goebbels kept up a press and radio campaign of exaggerations and outright lies. Ignoring the crushing effect of the two-front war and the barrage of mass-produced equipment coming from the Allies, he extolled their new secret weapons, the V1 and V2 rockets. "Germans," he exclaimed, "these super-weapons are going to carry us to victory! But remember, this is total war. We must carry on and fight whatever the cost!" The cost was great. Many families had lost a son, two sons, a husband or a father fighting on the Russian front or in the Balkans. Conditions inside and outside of Germany worsened. Various plots to assassinate Hitler were attempted unsuccessfully.

June, 1944 – The Germans people had become painfully aware that the struggle against the four powers vast superiority was hopeless. The Americans and British began a large scale campaign with airborne divisions landing in Normandy, and it looked like the Russians would soon launch an all-out offensive.

It seemed to Hitler that no matter what he did another threat always appeared. Sometimes it was almost more than he could bear. In spite of everything, he would never let anything or anyone stand in his way. Holding on to his grandiose ambitions gave him a temporary feeling that he was safe and in control. Accordingly, he continued to ignore pleas from his astrologers and generals to temporarily withdraw or surrender.

July 20, 1944 – "Afra, Afra!" She was outside in a futile search for food when she heard her neighbor call. "Turn on the wireless; they've thrown a bomb at Hitler!"

"What happened? Was he killed?" she shouted.

"I don't know, but it's on the wireless." Her neighbor hurried away,

It must have been the assassination attempt Afra had seen in Hitler's transits. She wondered if it succeeded. A surge of adrenalin ran through her body. She hurried up to the apartment and turned on the radio. A strained voice announced, "An attempt has been made on Hitler's life by Colonel Klaus von Stauffenberg and other conspirators. A bomb was placed in Hitler's headquarters. It exploded and killed his stenographer and wounded several people. We are grateful that Hitler's life has been spared."

When Hitler staggered out of the shambled building, his face was blackened, his hair stood up on his head like a bush, and his trousers were in shreds. He immediately telephoned Himmler. "I want everyone who is suspect hanged immediately!" he screamed with the demonical rage that was gaining increasing control over him. "Traitors!" he screamed. "You have sealed your fate! We'll drag you before the People's Court with lightning speed."

The first session of the Court sent Stauffenberg and eight other officers to the gallows. That night Hitler watched the naked men strangling in nooses made of piano wire suspended from meat hooks. Gloating, he savored their slow tortuous death. The consuming rage he felt against his father and everyone who opposed him escalated to massive retaliation. Over 4,000 people still awaited the death sentence.

Among them was Albrecht Haushofer, a young German Staff Major and son of Karl Haushofer. Once a convinced Nazi, he had become disillusioned when he grasped the real nature and extent of Hitler's personal ambitions. It didn't take long before he became aware that Germany had fallen into the hands of demonic powers.

For months he sat in Lehterstrasse Prison, deep in thought. What baffled Haushofer, a student of Oriental philosophy who had spent a year with the lamas in Tibet, was why Hitler was allowed to escape unharmed though his survival meant the prolonging of the war and the unbelievable destruction of Germany. Then, in a flash of intuition, he knew Hitler had to survive until Germany was totally over-run by her enemies. Only when every city, town and hamlet of the Fatherland was reduced to ruins and occupied by enemy troops could the entire population understand the ultimate consequence of permitting the Nazi regime to arise in their midst.

What amazed Haushofer even more was how the beneficent forces of light used the working of evil to realize their moral aims for humanity. While pondering these lines of thought he gained deep insight into how the Law of Karma molds the fate of an entire people.

When Himmler received the long lists of individuals Hitler suspected in plots against him, he spotted Afra Waesch's name. He respected her because she had saved his life by selecting a favorable time for his operation, but he knew that Hitler expected his commands to be carried out explicitly. Therefore he reluctantly included her name with his own orders. However, when the Gestapo, accompanied by Visser, arrived at her apartment, the place was deserted.

Fearing the worst, Afra and her family had left for Kassel to stay with her parents.

~~

As defeat loomed it was all Hitler could do to keep from falling into the depths of despair. He was surrounded with nothing but cowards, liars and traitors. There was no one he could trust. Everyone was against him! Everything he'd worked so hard for was crashing down. Still, he refused to give up. By taking action he would drive the terror back. He attempted to fill the ranks with the young and the old, children between twelve and eighteen and men between fifty and sixty. About half a million boys and older men were conscripted into military service.

August, 1944 — The Red Army bottled up fifty German divisions in the Baltic region and penetrated German occupied Finland. Rumania, the source of Germany's oil, surrendered to the Russians. Two days later, German occupied France was liberated.

September, 1944 – Russia declared war on Bulgaria and quickly conquered it. The German armies in France and the rest of Western Europe lost 500,000 men, half of them as prisoners, and almost all of their tanks, artillery and trucks. According to General Speidel, "We no longer have any ground forces in evidence, to say nothing of air forces."

When Hitler had to make great decisions, he often awoke with a hypnotic certainty that prompted him exactly what he had to do. But now he was so besieged with nightmares he was afraid to go to sleep. He kept all the lights on during the night and obliged his staff to sit through long monologues on topics such as war, history, astrology and the evils of eating meat. No matter what he did the horror of a nightmare would always close in on him.

"Who's that?" he cried out in the middle of his dream. He sat bolt upright, sweating profusely and shaking with so fearfully the bed vibrated. He began mumbling strange un-German words. After some moments they dwindled away. In the dim shadows stood the figure that had appeared to him so long ago during Dietrich Eckart's frightening ritual. Slowly its elegant facade dissolved revealing its true essence, a demon of monstrous size, black and hairy. Its features were gross and coarse. Its eyes were horrific. Sharp fangs protruded from its mouth.

"I'm he-e-e-r-e for you." The words came out in a mocking sneer.

Hitler cringed in his bed, wild and terrified by the demon looming before him. "You are mine forever," the demon gloated. Its glowing eyes burned red with hatred.

Hitler knew he no longer had freedom of choice. A world of horrors was closing in. Realizing he was on the edge of madness he let out a blood-curdling scream. Where the demon had been standing was empty space.

A servant heard him and rushed in. He saw his Fuhrer sitting on the bed shaking and panic stricken, fists clenched, lips blue. "He! He's been here!" Hitler gasped, his eyes wide with terror.

"Wake up, mein Fuhrer, wake up!" the servant cried. "It's just a bad dream."

Chapter 28

January 15, 1945 — After lunch with his staff of generals, secretaries, cooks, bodyguards and Dr. Morrell, Hitler left his command center in East Prussia and boarded his special train. They were bound for Berlin where he was going to relocate in the Fuhrer Bunker, a bombproof subterranean world fifty feet beneath the Chancellery garden. Covered with a massive canopy of reinforced concrete, the bunker had electricity, fresh water, kitchen and telephone exchange. The bottom floor housed Hitler, Joseph Goebbels and his family, Martin Bormann, and numerous generals.

March 19, 1945 — Hitler was in an optimistic mood. Hundreds of new jets were ready to go. Jet reconnaissance planes reopened the skies over England and Scotland. The first Mark XXI submarine set forth for US shores. Underground oil plants were being built by the SS. At least 5,452 Soviet tanks were claimed destroyed, and Soviet tank losses were outrunning production.

Then overnight Hitler's optimism took a plunge when he learned his own armies were suffering crippling shortages of weapons, ammunition and explosives. Virtually all aircraft production had ceased. The ground attack and air-transport squadrons were running out of replacement aircraft and tank brigades were running out of gasoline. One fifth of all essential medical items were unattainable, and two fifths more would be completely out of stock in a couple of months. Without medicines his people would be cut down by disease and epidemics. The vast sums of money and unheeding use of manpower to rebuild Berlin together with governmental corruption and an endless war had virtually stripped Germany of manpower and finances.

The advance on Russia had deteriorated to a trudging crawl. April 9th General Lasch surrendered to the Russians. Hitler shrieked, "General Lasch is to be shot as a traitor immediately!" He was locked in such fury that he seemed on the verge of madness, possessed by the Devil.

Then, as quick as his vicious burst of energy, he was overcome with fatigue. Secret fears and anxieties weighed him down with a feeling of hopelessness. He was deathly afraid of his nightmares, and at the same time afraid he'd lost the supernatural powers the demon had bestowed on him. He was afraid of illness, premature death, assassination by one of his associates, and the failure of his great mission.

Two days later he hunched over the command table, a slowly disintegrating lump. He struggled to pull himself together. The latest report informed him millions of British and American troops had landed on the French coast headed for Germany. How was he going to deal with it all? He knew the stress of overwhelming responsibilities was getting to him. His mind no longer seemed as sharp as before. It was hard to grasp details and statistics as he once had. His memory was fading.

He lay on his bed blaming everyone. His thoughts always returned to recrimination of the German soldiers for surrendering to the Russians. He took no responsibility for his mistake of sending thousands of them to their death in Russia.

He had ordered Eva Braun to stay away. But her whole being was wrapped up in her Fuhrer. Defying his orders, she arrived at the bunker unexpectedly. "Adolph," she said with vehemence, "I had to come back." When he was with her, when he talked to her, she felt as though she was the only person in his world. She smiled at him fondly, "You know my whole life is loving you. I want to be with you to the end."

He gave her one of his rare smiles. She was the only person left whom he could absolutely trust. Her comforting presence was a welcome respite from the agonizing events occurring above the bunker. Her cheerful compliance suited him perfectly. He'd never wanted an intellectual companion full of opinions because he'd never been able to carry on the give and take of a normal conversation. With Eva he could talk for hours, and she would just answer briefly or nod her head in sympathy.

But his nightmares were more frequent and violent. Eva became accustomed to his waking during the night and calling out to her. He woke her crying out, "I can't take it another minute!"

She ran from her room and tried to hold him in her arms. "There's no one here," she assured him. "It was only a dream."

He felt her warm breath on his cheek and the protective closeness of her body. He was awake but he could still feel the demon's dark presence. I might as well be dead, he thought. At least I'd be free of these horrifying nightmares.

Chapter 29

Afra, Lilo and Ricky had been in Kassel for five months. Afra was worried because it had been many weeks since she'd heard from Ellen and Yvonne. God knew where they're touring with the Special Services.

She didn't realize she'd miss Egon so much. She remembered the times they spent the day together – talking, cooking dinner, going to the movies. And she missed playing his piano, that seemed to free her inhibitions and allowed her to unreservedly express her love and passion for him. She spoke from her heart through her music.

It was time to return to Berlin.

However, she quickly saw that life in the big city had deteriorated further. The bombing of industrial sites and losses of manpower and equipment were putting a tremendous strain on the economy. Food supplies were even more reduced and the quality was dreadful. Everyone, except the Nazis and soldiers, were undernourished. Most of the buses and tramlines were discontinued. Weary from ongoing rounds of bombings, hungry and in poor health, Berliners' morale had sunk to an all time low. To make matters worse, Afra had an awful foreboding something terrible was going to happen.

Still, she was filled with anticipation to see Egon again. As soon as she was settled, she made her way through piles of rubble to his apartment. With a chilling shock, she stared into the empty space where his building once stood. It had been flattened by Allied air raids. She asked a raggedy man shifting through the ruins. "Was anyone killed?"

He looked at her with weary eyes. "I'm afraid so. Fraulein. Six people were killed in the basement when the ceiling collapsed."

"Egon Beyer?" she whispered.

The man nodded sadly and returned to his hopeless task.

Afra sat on a chunk of broken cement, struck with shock and grief. Tears trickled down her cheeks. "Egon, my poor Egon," she moaned. He had been her friend, her mentor, her beloved. Now her world was an unbearable burden. Her head dropped and her shoulders crumbled with the weight and pain of it all.

Back at the apartment, she thought she couldn't take Hitler and his awful war a minute longer. She felt she'd burst from the storm of emotion that was building inside her since Hitler and his Nazis had taken over every facet of life. They were blocking her way in everything she tried to do.

But it wasn't just her. Hitler was using the German people, the Jews and conquered people like slaves, all for his own selfish benefit. The devastation, suffering and death he had caused spread throughout Europe. Words exploded in her mind. Damn you, Hitler! She wished he were dead, just so they could get on with their lives in peace.

She decided to go to the mountains for a few days. Throwing a few things into her valise, she said a hasty goodbye to Lilo and Ricky and stalked out of the apartment. The long hard walk to the station was but a further annoyance. The train was late, and then moved like a sluggish old turtle.

It was a relief when she arrived at the little hotel in the mountain village. The air was clean and refreshing and she was once more able to breathe deeply. In the evening, she took a short walk along a hillside trail. The long dusk faded into night. She looked up at the sky searching for guidance from the heavens. Distant flashes caught her eye, and she heard the sounds of bombs battering Berlin. How many people were going die that night? Would her family be safe?

Her moment of serenity was gone. She caught the last train back to the city. At Potsdam the train stopped, bombs had damaged the rails ahead. Everyone disembarked, scattering in various directions. She stood alone and stranded in front of the dark and deserted station. In the distance it looked as if a thousand bombers were streaming over Berlin. Searchlights swung back and forth through the night sky, reaching up nine thousand meters to find enemy planes. A bomber was struck by anti-aircraft guns and slashed down through the darkness in a burst of flame. Fires glowed on the horizon.

"Frau Waesch, WHAT are you doing out here?" A dirty jeep with Klaus Haffner, a former client, and another young soldier stopped right in front of her.

"Klaus, I'm so glad you came by!" Afra exclaimed in surprise. "Thank you for stopping. The train isn't going any farther, and it's urgent that I get to Berlin."

"We're on our way there. Please get in. We'd be pleased to have you ride with us, Frau Waesch. This is my friend, Fritz."

"*Guten abend*, Frau Waesch," Fritz greeted her as he jumped out of the jeep to hold the door open.

"*Guten abend*, Fritz." He took her valise and they climbed in. The jeep's engine accelerated. They pulled away from the isolated train station.

"Klaus and Fritz, your fortuitous arrival is a blessing. I could have been left standing there all night."

They drove through darkened villages and country streets, the lights of the searchlights flickering through the trees. Upon entering Berlin they saw the city had become a nightmarish hell.

Everything was burning. Dead bodies lay in the streets. Screams pierced the air. Afra was clutched with fear as they lurched their way through a valley of rubble, the remnants of apartment buildings. The drive was taking forever.

Like a miracle, her building stood before them amidst the ruins. "Look, look!" she cried. "It's still there!" They pulled up in front of the building, and she turned to her companions. "I'm so grateful to you both." Valise in hand, she stepped out of the jeep and ran up the steps. The door flew open and there were Lilo and Ricky with arms outstretched to greet her.

The next evening the lights went off. "Oh no!" cried Afra and Lilo in unison. "We might as well go to bed." Electricity was only coming on for minutes at a time. Water was limited, and the toilets didn't flush. When she went to the grocery store she had to stand in line with fifty or more women. After living through relentless air raids for three and a half years everyone's nerves were in shreds.

Afra remembered Berlin before the war — how clean and neat it was. Six days a week hundreds of street sweepers wearing octagon shaped hats with visors cleaned the city streets. Housewives scrubbed the steps to their front doors. Birds sang and fluttered about in miniature gardens.

Now everyone in Germany was in the same terrible predicament. So far she had been able to retain her German stoicism under all the adversities that befell them, but now she wondered if all the misery and devastation Hitler had caused would ever go away. Her long held self control changed into furious resentment. Perhaps praying would allow her to release the hopelessness that pervaded her soul.

Pasch's voice floated to her on glowing particles of light. "Afra, Afra, I am here to help you."

A blessing! Her angel was always on hand to comfort and guide her.

"Your prayers are more like grievances than an appeal to God. Afra, do you truly want to pray?"

"Yes, Pasch."

"Then you must first of all love your enemies. Putting all of your attention on Hitler and his cohorts is a problem because they aren't going to do what you want. They can only be themselves. The biggest test is to love people who are the most unlovable, even those who have done many cruel, inhumane things."

How hard that is, she thought in despair. What the Nazis have done is unforgivable.

"Afra, you must let go of the past. Only by releasing the anger and bitterness you've built up against Hitler and other harmful people will you find peace of mind." He spoke softly. "Hatred and animosity are born out of unfulfilled desires and a need for things to be right as you see it. You must let go of all that. You must pray for Hitler and send him your light and love. In this way your heart will become more open. You will have inspiration to do higher things.   And at one fortunate point the light will shine within and outside you."

He slowly faded away, until all that remained was her memory of his eyes full of peace, tranquility and love.

As always her guardian angel's magical presence gave her a ray of hope. She began to relax. She closed her eyes. Her mind became quiet. The anger she had clung to so avidly was released. Forgiveness and love flooded her heart and flew out to Hitler. She knew at last it was possible that even the most hated — the most unlovable — could be loved.

Pasch's words filled her mind. "Now you know what praying really is."

After that day her life became lighter. Instead of seeing everything as wrong, everything suddenly felt right. She couldn't have explained it, but she knew with a certainty there was a higher evolutionary purpose to everything seemingly dark and dismal.

Lilo was also happier. During the long months of Brandt Wilhelm's recovery, they had become good friends. Brandt was genial, kind and devotedly loyal to his memories of Richard, and it was easy for her to be in his company. In fact, Brandt acquired an growing circle of friends and acquaintances. The day he was discharged he was offered a job as a mechanic. Walking with a cane didn't faze him in the least.

By this time Lilo discovered there was a lot more to him than appeared on the surface. Underneath a down to earth and unpretentious personality, he was a hard worker, sturdy and blessed with great fortitude. He'd grown on her until she realized she wanted to be with him always. In time their friendship blossomed into love.

Chapter 30

1945 -- Arcs of light streamed from exploding shells, flashing on clouds in the dark sky. Afra and her family ran toward the bomb shelter and scrambled down the stairs to safety. Close behind was Brandt, quick on his feet despite the use of a cane. Once inside the entrance to the shelter, they turned to assist Afra. But she was nowhere in sight.

Unbeknownst to them, she tripped and fell down two blocks before. Shaken but unhurt, she struggled to her feet. She heard a chilling voice.

"I've got you now."

She turned quickly and found herself facing Visser. Flames from a burning house barely lit up the outline of his head. Ice-cold fear raced down her spine, while rooftop gargoyles gazed on the scene with stony indifference. Visser's face seemed to have elongated; there were deep lines between his eyebrows and from his nostrils to the sides of his mouth. His eyes were black pits. He seemed to be consumed with directing all of his Nazi hate toward her.

Suddenly out of nowhere, a strange man on a bicycle flew around the corner and knocked him down.

"Dumkopf!" cried Visser, locked in a tangle of bicycle and man.

Taking advantage the situation, Afra ran down an alley and turned into the next street. She looked over her shoulder and saw Visser following her from a distance. She forced herself to run faster, desperately looking for a place to hide. Ah, there's an alleyway, she thought. Slipping into it, she quieted her breathing: just listening. In the distance was the dull thudding of bombs landing, but there were no sounds of Visser's running footsteps. She stared at the dark walls and blacked out windows surrounding her. What am I doing here? she wondered. Hunted down by a crazy man when I should be home with my family. Cautiously she peeked out. Visser was nowhere in sight.

Hurrying from one hiding place to the next, she headed in the general direction of the bomb shelter and her family. She strode around a burned-out car and came face to face with a dark figure before her. Her pulse quickened.

The man reached out as if to steady himself. "I'm sorry," he stammered, and went on his way. Perhaps he was drunk, perhaps he was sick or injured.

She finally got back to the street where the bomb shelter was located. As she turned the corner, her pursuer loomed in front of her in the black night. She knew he would kill her.

"So you thought you could get away from me, you silly fool," he mocked.

"Please! Please!" she cried out. If only she were back with her family.

"Oh no, I've got you now, Frau Waesch!" he screamed. He raised a heavy riding whip and swung a crushing blow to her head that sent her reeling to the ground. Towering over her he lashed out with the whip again and again. It was the talisman of power that he had stolen from the Fuhrer's office. "You're nobody!" he laughed harshly.

She moaned, but searing pain rendered her unable to move, her head angled awkwardly to one side.

Visser grabbed her shoulders with both hands, banging her head, drenching the cobblestone pavement with blood. Panting hard and fast, he stopped and lowered his head inches from her face to see if she was still alive. Mucus hung from his nose. With each inhalation it made bubbling sounds. He saw she was still breathing. The mucus fell and slid down her cheek. With a scornful smile, Visser roughly rubbed it into her face. He looked around anxiously, but there were no witnesses.

He stood up and dragged her to a thick stone wall fronting a street fifteen feet below. Disregarding the blood pouring from her head, mouth and ears he lifted her on top of it to push her over the edge. He climbed onto the wall and stood over her limp body, master at last. He knelt and used his fingers soaked with her blood to pry her eyes open. But they were vacant. Afra was somewhere else.

"Look at me!" he demanded. "I want you to know. You're dead, bitch!" Suddenly he was interrupted by a serene yet commanding voice behind him.

"Herr Visser, it is not her time to die."

Startled and confused, Visser abruptly stood and awkwardly spun around. Hovering before him in mid-air was Afra's guardian angel. Visser jumped back a little, lost his balance and, shrieking in horror, fell from the wall to the street below. He landed headfirst with a sickening thud, his mouth a hole of disbelief. Hitler's whip lay in his dead hand.

Brandt deposited Lilo and Ricky in the bomb shelter and went outside to search for Afra. He found her just as a jeep pulled up with two soldiers. They gently lifted Afra into the vehicle and sped off to the hospital.

Brandt returned to Lilo and Ricky. As soon as the air raid was over, they lost no time heading for the hospital. It took them over an hour to walk there through all the rubble and potholes. Along the way, Lilo cried in anguish. She feared the worst.

At the hospital, as they tiptoed into her room, they saw her entire head was covered with bandages. Although her eyes were red, her complexion was pallid, and her face was battered and swollen. She lay in a deep coma.

A nurse escorted them to the doctor's office. "I'm Doctor Schafer," he introduced himself. "We're doing all we can. Frau Waesch has severe head injuries and a concussion. She requires surgery to relieve swelling of the brain and any blood clots that could cause brain damage." A frown momentarily flickered on his face. "Her condition is critical. She might not survive surgery. And, if we are able to save her, she may have mental and physical disabilities related to brain damage." He paused, knowing what a difficult time this was for them. "I need your permission to proceed with the surgery."

Lilo choked, inhaled with a gasp. She nodded her head in agreement with the doctor. Brandt could tell by the defeated look in the doctor's eyes that he had little, if any, hope for Afra's recovery.

As soon as Lilo signed the forms, Dr. Schafer and his surgical team took over. They wheeled her to surgery, prepped her, and gave her anesthesia. After the operation Dr. Schafer spoke to Lilo. "I succeeded in removing the blood clots but she is still comatose." He saw the alarmed look on her face and hurried on, "Please don't worry. She's been through a lot of trauma and needs to be quiet for a while." He gave her a reassuring smile. "But even while comatose she can hear every word you say. Tell her you love her and that she will recover completely and soon."

Ellen returned home from her last tour. She and Lilo were spending time every day at the hospital. One day Ellen was sitting by the bed holding her mother's hand. Lilo was nearby reading a book. Brandt was home with Ricky.

Afra unexpectedly opened her eyes. Her head was throbbing painfully, relentlessly. Turning it with utmost care, she saw she was in a room she didn't recognize. Ellen held her hand. "Where am I?" she asked softly.

"Oh Mutti," Ellen exclaimed, "you're here in the hospital with us." She squeezed her hand, and Lilo rushed over. Crying for joy, they cautiously kissed her cheek. Afra tried her best to ignore her aching head. She managed a weak smile and asked for a sip of water.

The next day she sat up. The pain in her head was just bearable. She smiled at her daughters sitting by her. "We're so glad to have you back," Lilo said. "You've been in a coma for two weeks."

Remembering her awful encounter with Visser, Afra assured them, "You will never know how good it is to see you. I want you to tell me everything that's been happening. But first I must get up for a bit. I feel really stiff. Could I take a look outside?"

Even with Ellen and Lilo supporting her, it took a huge effort for Afra to move her legs and sit up. Finally she was standing, and the girls walked her to the window. They looked down on a barren landscape of demolished buildings. Suddenly bright sunshine broke through the clouds. The darkness that had engulfed her on that terrible night when Visser attacked her was gone. She began to come to life again in the warm rays of the sun.

"We have a surprise for you, Mutti," said Ellen, a broad smile on her face.

"Oh yes!" agreed Lilo. "Today is April 10th. Your birthday. It's your birthday!"

In unison, they exclaimed, "Happy birthday, our beloved Mutti!"

It was a glorious day she would never forget.

Chapter 31

The air raids kept getting worse. Sometimes it appeared as though the whole city was on fire. The sounds of rumbling of artillery were unceasing. Soldiers marched, and endless lines of people walked or pushed carts filled with belongings. Dead horses, dogs and people lay on the streets. Russian soldiers raped women and looted. German deserters hung from lampposts as traitors.

Holed up in his bunker, Hitler tensed every time the ground shook from bombs dropped by 1,000 British and Americans planes staging their last massive raid on Berlin. Simultaneously 1,500 Russian tanks and 12,700 Russian mortars attacked the city.

Yet Hitler was still unyieldingly stubborn. He continued to sacrifice his defense positions, fortifications and whole divisions. Refusing to accept defeat he told Albert Speer, "I cannot turn back."

During a temporary lull Hitler, Eva, Himmler, Goebbels, Borman and a few military chiefs made their way up for their Fuhrer's birthday party. They assembled in a ruined room at the Chancellery to shake his hand in a demonstration of loyalty. No one quite knew what to say. Shortly thereafter they returned to the bunker. It was hard to see him, a beaten man – a physical wreck with shaking head and grasping a limp left arm with a trembling hand.

"Albert," Hitler said, finally aware that all was lost, "this is the end of our great plans. I want nothing left. I want you to oversee the destruction of what remains of Germany. All military installations, communications, bridges, railways, electrical facilities, water and gas works, food and clothing stores. All must be destroyed."

Speer looked at his Fuhrer's bloodshot eyes and chalky skin and finally awakened to his insanity. As soon Speer left the bunker he went about the task of countermanding as many of Hitler's orders as he could.

During this time both Goering and Himmler, whose loyalty Hitler had completely trusted, deserted the bunker. Independent of each other, they were negotiating to make a separate peace with the Western Powers wherein they would govern Germany. Hitler cursed them wildly and immediately sent for Colonel von Grein. "I want you to arrest them both!" he ordered. "I will not allow either of them to succeed me!"

Hitler to the end saw things only in black or white. He was Germany's great leader and conqueror — or the victim of fools, traitors, and the German people who let him down.

A gray haze of smoke hung over Berlin. People cried out in fear as Russian artillery shells fell randomly. Russian soldiers brandished their Victory Banner from the roof of the Reichstag. Russians tanks rumbled over the pavement, slowly closing in on the Fuhrer's bunker.

Hitler could no longer deny the death of the Third Reich. Everyone except Eva had betrayed him.

He said to her, "During all my years of struggle I knew I had to devote all my efforts to my cause. Now Eva, after many years of friendship, I've decided to take you as my wife."

She agreed. For the wedding she made herself up carefully with bright lipstick, rouge and penciled eyebrows. She selected Hitler's favorite dress from her elegant wardrobe. It was black silk with a bell-shaped skirt, two roses set in a deep neckline, and a trim bolero. Hitler wore an olive gray shirt and black trousers. On his chest he wore his gold party badge and the Iron Cross he had won in the Great War.

At the appointed hour against the drone of whirring fans in the bunker, they became man and wife in a hurried ceremony. Eva made a pretty picture, but Hitler had become an old man with trembling hands and a slow shuffling walk. Although he was finally committing himself to another person, he had never felt so hopelessly depressed and lonely – like a stranger unknown to anyone and himself.

Later, he said to Eva, "Germany is doomed. As Fuhrer I would be blamed for everything." Feeling life leaving him, he gave a sigh of resignation. "I ask you, my faithful companion, to die with me. Escape the ultimate disgrace of failure and the contempt of defeat."

Eva trembled but had never deviated in her devotion to her Fuhrer. "Adolph, you know I've always loved you. My only wish is to share your fate."

On April 30, 1945 they said their last farewells to those who still remained in the bunker and went to his suite. Eva placed a shawl over the lamp softening the light. They sat on the sofa and Hitler whispered, "Take the pill on the table, Eva. It will make the ending quiet."

Tears rolled down her cheeks. She picked up the glass and swallowed the poison. "Good-bye, Adolph," she said as she lay back on the sofa and closed her eyes. Her hands lay quietly in her lap – she knew her husband did not like to be touched. Her breathing diminished and finally stopped.

Hitler looked upon the woman who had remained faithful to the end. Everyone else had abandoned him. Germany was defeated. He had become successful beyond his wildest dreams, but now his power was gone. He had lost everything. The humiliation was more than he could bear. He was nothing but a miserable failure.

He picked up his gun. Put it to his temple, and pulled the trigger.

EPILOGUE

May 7, 1945 – The war ended. Millions of young German men had died in blind obedience to Hitler.

Berliners emerged from cellars, shelters and subway tunnels, hoping they could get on with their lives.

In Nuremberg members of the American 7th Army unlocked a huge vault hidden nine hundred feet below a medieval castle. Stunned, they stared in silence before plundered riches beyond compare: paintings, art treasures, priceless antiquities and jewels. Resting on top of a ten-foot altar was a worn leather case containing Hitler's most prized possession, the Spear of Destiny.

Later the Spear was transferred back to the Hapsburg Treasure House where Hitler first beheld it in 1909.

The Americans took over the sector where Afra and her family lived. Ellen and Yvonne wasted no time contacting the American Social Services to book their dance act. Soon they were performing for American soldiers. After every show they joined the military staff for dinner. They dug into the biggest and most delicious meals they had eaten in years. Ellen had her fork poised over a big piece of apple pie, when Captain John Roy, said to her. "Well, Fraulein, I see you have a good healthy appetite."

"I'm only making up for lost time, Captain Roy. I can't remember when our basic staples were more than potatoes and ersatz coffee." She had already noticed him – tall, straight shouldered and intelligent, a conqueror.

Eventually Ellen married John, and Yvonne married a sergeant named Bob Williams. Ellen and John moved to San Diego, California; Yvonne and Bob to Coeur D'Alene, Idaho. Lilo, Brandt and Ricky settled in Munich, Brandt's hometown.

In 1946 Afra went to stay with her parents in Kassel. Her mother lay quietly in bed, pale and very ill. After several months she died peacefully in her sleep.

Afra began doing horoscopes, but everything had changed. The Reichmark was practically worthless.

In 1950 her father passed away, leaving her a nice inheritance. Suddenly her life opened up. Now she could be with Ellen in California.

She found a spacious apartment in San Diego. Sunlight poured in from wide windows. A deck overlooked the ocean. In that warm, peaceful setting she thought about her life in Germany and the consequences of Hitler's terrible regime. Many books about the war had come out, none from an astrologer's viewpoint. She would write about the war, the German people, Hitler and his band of Nazis. *Can It Happen Again?* was the title she chose for her book.

As she summed up her conclusions, she recalled what Egon had said to her, "Imagine how things would have been if all of Germany, if the whole world had been coming from a place of peace and love. Only with love and worldwide cooperation is it possible to transcend barriers of nationality, race and culture. Only then will we be able to achieve lasting peace."

Afra wrote:

Although Hitler's anger drove him to achieve his ambitions with force and terror, it never works to compromise with evil. It's frightening to think another world war could happen again, for many people believe nothing can be accomplished except by domination and fighting. Unfortunately, they're usually unaware the real battle-ground is within us. We must face our own internal dark side and bring our negative thoughts into harmony. Then the guiding light in our own souls will reflect on others and lead us into the coming Age of Peace.

She found a publisher for her book. She was increasingly content living in her new home. The war, Hitler, the hunger and the cold winters were long ago and far away. Now there was only warm sunshine and blue skies. Breezes moved the palm trees. Clouds lingered on the ocean's edge. The sun slipped into the water. She realized she was happier then she had ever been.

One late afternoon while lounging in her deck chair, out of the corner of her eye she saw a flash of light. It was Pasch encircled in glowing luminosity.

"Dear One, do you remember when I told you someday the sun would shine in your heart?"

She nodded, knowing this was an important visit indeed.

"By facing so many setbacks and tribulations you've come to that place of peace, forgiveness, and loving acceptance. Now it's time to take the road homeward with me." He held out his hand. She instantly took it. He pulled her rapidly through a long tunnel. Ahead in the darkness she could see light. But before they had gone very far, Pasch stopped. They stepped into a hidden alcove. He opened a door. They descended into a shadowy place of darkness.

Before them a continuous stream of washed out beings, heads and shoulders hunched, walking aimlessly. This must be what they call Hell, she thought. She noticed a spirit moving with slow, shuffling steps, dragging his right leg, bent over and locked in hopeless despair. The ashen gray hair hanging over his forehead reminded her of Hitler. Why am I here? Afra wondered, feeling she was only part way to somewhere else.

Pasch answered her unspoken question. "You needed to see what happens to the lost souls who forego God for self-willed ego. Bound by attachments, they're caught between the spiritual and material worlds. Until they give up anger, hatred and unforgiveness, putting themselves in God's hands, they can't go to the other side. Still, even if it takes many lifetimes, in the end everybody goes to the Light."

She saw that each of the souls contained a tiny star of light.

After what seemed an eternity, she turned to Pasch, followed his upward gaze and saw the shadows dissolve. Like flying birds, they rose effortlessly through yielding clouds into the blue sky. Music was all around, filling her soul with boundless graceful harmony and changing themes.

Beyond, the heavens were flooded with Light. Swiftly, they moved closer. Afra was completely surrounded by the Light of indescribable Beauty, Peace and Happiness. She knew she was with God – bathed in love beyond compare. She was home.

APPENDIX

ASTROLOGICAL GLOSSARY

AFFLICTED: Generally refers to a planet with inharmonious aspects, particularly conjunctions to a malefic planet, squares or oppositions.

AIR SIGNS: Gemini, Libra and Aquarius are mental types, as thoughts travel through the air. They want to communicate with others, to be part of their activities and to make them part of theirs. They are clever but lack warmth and sympathy.

ASCENDANT: The degree of the zodiac that appears on the horizon at the moment of birth. The Ascendant is one of the important factors in the horoscope, because it shows the native's outlook on life. Therefore, it colors the whole interpretation of the chart.

ASPECT: The aspects depict the flow of force between the planets. The planets influence each other harmoniously or inharmoniously according to the angle, or aspect, they form with each other. The results of the aspects are not always obvious, for they work on the physical, mental, emotional or spiritual level.

<u>Conjunction</u> This aspect means close together, meaning two or more planets within no more than 10 degrees of each other. The conjunction gives a blending of the qualities of the planets involved that is favorable or unfavorable depending on the planets themselves and their aspects. Hitler has Venus and Mars exactly conjunct in Taurus.

<u>Sextile</u> The sextile is about 60 degrees and is a mental aspect. It shows how the native thinks on subjects of interest to him. It is creative in expression and inclines to wide social contacts. It brings opportunities through effort. Hitler has one sextile, Saturn sextiles Uranus.

Square means one planet is approximately 90 degrees from another one. Square aspects often denote achievement because they give force and energy to overcome obstacles and get things done whether the intentions are good or bad. However, squares also indicate the probability of misdirected action and a disregard for rules and regulations. If the native doesn't learn how to transmute the square and expresses its negative or destructive side, he pays for it. He won't get away with anything where the squares are concerned. The closest square in the chart shows where he puts the most effort. Hitler has Venus and Mars squaring Saturn, clearly showing his rise and fall.

Trine is approximately 120 degrees. Trines bring good luck. They give an easy flow of expression. Therefore, many trines can make a person lazy. If there aren't any strong squares, this individual often sits back and doesn't accomplish very much. Opportunities are brought to him, but he lets them slip by. With many trines in the chart, he can get away with a lot. Hitler has the Sun trine Jupiter and the Moon and Jupiter make wide trines to Venus and Mars.

Inconjunct is approximately 150 degrees. Only a 3 degree orb is allowed. Although it's considered a minor aspect, it's an important one. It's an aspect of adjustment. It's a substitution, or the taking away of something. The inconjunct has to do with health, employment, death and sex. Hitler has Venus and Mars in Taurus inconjunct Uranus indicating a sexual problem or substitution. He also has the Moon inconjunct Pluto in the 8th House of sex.

Opposition is approximately 180 degrees. It involves two planets opposed to each other having to do with relationships because oppositions are opposing forces. Thus, there are apt to be conflicts with other people. The solution is to find a balance in the middle by becoming aware of what is going on at each end of the opposition. Rohm has five oppositions, indicating many relationship problems.

ASTROLOGY: An occult science that studies the cosmic forces emanating from the Sun, Moon and planets and their relationship to each other and how this affects people.

BENEFIC PLANETS: Jupiter is the greater benefic planet and Venus is the lesser benefic.

BUCKET CHART: One of seven Planetary Patterns. Nine planets fall within 180 degrees and the 10th planet lies opposite them like the handle to the bucket. Or, as in the case of Goring, when two planets are conjunct within a degree making the handle. The "handle" planet(s) is a high focus with its effect very much emphasized.

CARDINAL: Aries, Cancer, Libra and Capricorn. The Cardinal type person is active and always has something to do. Goring, a Capricorn, has five planets in Cardinal Signs.

DIGNITY & DETRIMENT: A planet is dignified when it is in a sign in which it is able to express its own special qualities easily. For example, Mars is "at home" in Scorpio, but Hitler has Mars in the opposite sign Taurus. Mars afflicted in Taurus can give obsession for money and material things, as well as violence arising from sexual jealousy.

There is another aspect to the dignities and debilities. Each planet has a particular sign apart from the one it rules in which it expresses its nature in the very best way. The exaltations are seen at their very best when the individual is highly evolved. The Sun is exalted in Aries. Whereas the average person with the Sun in Aries has high vitality and a strong individuality, the evolved Arian is able to express the solar spiritual energy in its highest form. Afra has the Sun in Aries.

When a planet is in the sign opposite its exalted position, it's "in fall." Therefore, the Sun is in fall in Libra, the sign opposite Aries. The native has a weak ego and must step aside for the sake of the other person. Himmler has the Sun in Libra.

Hitler and many of the Nazi leaders described in this book have the Moon in detriment or fall.

EARTH SIGNS: Taurus, Virgo and Capricorn. Earth signs are basically interested in tangible values. If there are many planets in earth signs, the native may be mercenary in his concern over the material things of life. Hitler has five planets in earth signs.

EPHEMERIS: A book giving the computed positions of the planets for every day of one year or as long as one hundred years.

FALL: See Dignity.

FATED DEGREE: The 29th degree is a fated degree. It indicates misfortune connected with the planet. Himmler has Saturn and Neptune in fated degrees.

FIRE SIGNS: Aries, Leo and Sagittarius. The fire type person is self-sufficient, individualistic, self-expressive, ardent and forceful with a sense of adventure. Rohm, a Sagittarian, was the only Nazi leader who was a fire sign. He was the only one who had the guts to tell Hitler off. Hitler eventually took care of that by having him executed.

FIXED SIGNS: Taurus, Leo, Scorpio and Aquarius. The native with many fixed signs has fixity of purpose and once he makes up his mind about anything, he is difficult, perhaps impossible, to sway or change. Hitler has four planets in fixed signs.

FIXED STARS: The early astronomers divided the celestial bodies into two groups, the fixed stars and the erratic or wandering stars that we now call planets. Actually, the so-called fixed stars are not really fixed: they are traveling through space at tremendous speed, but because they are millions of miles away they appear to be stationary. As a rule astrologers don't bother with the fixed stars because they are beyond our solar system and only minimally affect the average chart.

Planetary effects are usually gradual and work comparatively slowly. But when a planet acts suddenly and drastically for no obvious reason, it's likely that a fixed star is operating somewhere in the background through the planet involved. However, keep in mind that the fixed stars cannot imbue a person with a quality that is not shown in the chart, meaning they affect and exaggerate only the planetary influences already in the chart.

Because of the malefic nature and aspects of the fixed stars in the Nazi leaders' charts, they threw these men up to a great height and then flung them down abruptly, bringing a series of losses, disgrace and unforeseen disaster.

Hitler, Geli Raubel and Eva Braun (two of the women in Hitler's life) have planets conjunct Facies, the star most often configured where crime, murder, suicide and violent death are concerned. The question is, did Geli Raubel commit suicide or did Hitler have her murdered because he couldn't control her? Eva Braun once tried to commit suicide and later did commit suicide with Hitler.

GRAND TRINE: A Grand Trine is a configuration composed of three or more planets in trine aspect to each other so they form a triangle. The emphasis of trines brings good luck without much effort, so that confidence is innate (at least in the area covered by the Grand Trine). But since trines don't give energy, it is best when there are one or more strong squares to support them. Afra has a Grand Trine with the Sun, Jupiter and Ascendant.

HOROSCOPE: The natal chart set up for the hour, date and place of birth. It shows the native's potentials and the trends of his life.

HOUSES: The wheel is divided into twelve houses that show the environment and circumstances through which the planets manifest. Each house depicts a department of life, and the planets in a house signify what kind of activity is going on there.

When there are planets in a house, there is more activity there. For example, Hitler has the Sun, Venus and Mars in the Seventh House of other people. What he did to the world, the world did back to him.

INTERCEPTED SIGNS: The tilt of the Earth on its axis often distorts house sizes if the birthplace is far north or south of the equator. When this happens, a sign may be completely contained within the house so it doesn't appear on any cusp. This is called an intercepted sign. Adolph Hitler has the Moon intercepted in Capricorn in the 3rd House of communication.

When he expounded his bitter feelings about the Versailles Treaty and the Jews he held his audience under his spell.

MALEFIC PLANETS: This term was popular with the old school fatalistic type of astrologers. The malefics are Saturn the reaper, Mars the trouble maker, Uranus the revolutionary, Neptune the deceiver and Pluto the destroyer. On the positive side, Mars is action and initiative, Saturn is discipline and structure, Uranus is universal love, Neptune is imagination and Pluto is regeneration and transformation.

MC: The Medium Coeli or Midheaven. This is the 10th House cusp.

MUTABLE SIGNS: Gemini, Virgo, Sagittarius and Pisces. The mutable person is adaptable.

NODES: The Moon's nodes are points where the orbit of the Moon intercepts the ecliptic. The North Node is where the Moon crosses the ecliptic going North. It is represented in the chart by a symbol that looks like a little hook as used in sewing. The South Node is where the Moon crosses the Ecliptic going South. It's opposite the north node and the hook is upside down. The South Node shows subconscious habit patterns from past lifetimes that should be outgrown. The north node points to the way one should go in the present life.

Hitler has the South Node in Capricorn testifying that in past incarnations he was self-centered, acquisitive and ambitious. As a carryover, in his life as a dictator he was a cold and calculating opportunist, allowing no weakness to prevent the attainment of a goal he had set his sights on. His North Node in Cancer means that he needed to develop qualities of sensitivity and emotion. In past lives he was a taker, in his Nazi life his challenge was to give.

PLANETARY PATTERNS: The seven planetary patterns give a general prototype of the native's temperament or self-expression. They are like an overview before we break the horoscope down into signs, planets, houses, aspects and so forth. The only planetary pattern delineated in this book is the Bucket. Many horoscopes do not come under any Planetary Pattern.

PLANETS: Any heavenly body that shines by reflected sunlight and revolves around the Sun. The major planets are Mercury, Venus, Earth, Mars, Jupiter, Saturn, Uranus, Neptune and Pluto.

☿   ♀   ♂   ♃   ♄   ♅   ♆   ♇

Mercury Venus Mars Jupiter Saturn Uranus Neptune Pluto

☉   ☽

In astrology, we include the Sun and Moon as planets.

PROGRESSIONS: This is a chart erected for the date that is as many days after birth as the native is in years. Progressions indicate when planetary influences shown in the natal chart come into being. If the potential is shown in the horoscope, progressions often bring in major events in the life.

RETROGRADE PLANETS: This is a term applied to an apparent backward motion of a planet when decreasing in longitude as viewed from the Earth. It can be compared to the effect of watching a slow moving car as seen from another car faster moving car that is traveling along with it. The slower moving car seems to be moving backward.

When a planet is direct in motion, the characteristics attributed to it move forward into action in a free flowing way. But when a planet is retrograde, the energy of the particular planet seems to circle around and go back into the unconscious. If negative, thoughts or emotions are held within, the mind and feelings can become diseased. Hitler has Venus retrograde.

Retrograde planets also have a karmic effect; events from a former life that still have a hold on the individual.

SIGNS: There are twelve signs in the zodiac: Aries, Taurus, Gemini, Cancer, Leo, Virgo, Libra, Scorpio, Sagittarius, Capricorn, Aquarius and Pisces. The characteristics of the planets are expressed through the sign that they appear in.

The three most important factors in the horoscope are the Sun that depicts the real you, your individuality and your will; the

Moon that depicts your subconscious, your feelings and your ability to connect with others; and the Ascendant.

SUN SIGNS

♈ **Aries** ... March 21 – April 20: Key phrase "I am." Aries natives are driven to express their individuality in their own way. Their energies are apt to be self-centered and self-directed. Symbolized by a red hot flame that quickly flares up and quickly goes out, they have short but fierce enthusiasms. Cardinal/fire.

♉ **Taurus** ... April 21 – May 20: Key phrase "I have." Earthy and materialistic, Taurus is the sign of ownership. These natives want more than ample wealth and possessions as tangible symbols of security. The basic lesson is to learn a true sense of values. Once Taureans get going, they have great fixity of purpose and build forever. Fixed/earth.

♊ **Gemini** ... May 21 – June 21: Key phrase "I think." Gemini carries thoughts and communication through the air. Like the breeze, Geminis flit around here and there to experience and grow. They may have little to show for their efforts, if they never settle down.   Mutable/air.

♋ **Cancer** ... June 22 – July 21: Key phrase "I feel." Symbolized by the restless tides of the ocean, Cancer expresses the surging and ebbing of emotion. If emotions are allowed to run rampant, reason goes out the window. Cancer is the mothering, nurturing sign of the zodiac.   Cardinal/water.

♌ **Leo** ... July 22 – August 21: Key phrase "I will." Symbolized by the Sun, the center of the solar system, Leos want to be the center of their world. They relish being in control. However, their lesson is "God's will, not mine, be done." Like the eternal Sun, Leos can be depended on. Fixed/fire.

♍ **Virgo** ... August 22 – September 21: Key phrase "I serve."   Virgos are practical by nature; they find their fullest expression through service to others. They take care of all the details that other signs overlook. Nevertheless, they may miss the main issue and need to avoid nit picking over minor details. Mutable/earth.

♎ **Libra** … September 22 – October 21: Key phrase "I balance." Libra is the sign of marriage and partnership, and Librans seek balance and harmony in relationships and in every phase of life. They want beautiful surroundings, love and peace, but need to guard against a tendency toward compromise and "peace at any price." Cardinal/air.

♏ **Scorpio** … October 22 – November 21: Key phrase "I desire." Scorpio is the most extreme of all the signs. These people are seldom moderate, and consequently their powerful desires can lead to remarkable achievement or total destruction. Their challenge is to transmute baser desires. Fixed/water.

♐ **Sagittarius** ... November 22 – December 21: Key phrase "I see." Sagittarius has a wonderful ability to see many possibilities and opportunities, especially through long distance travel, both physically and mentally. Like embers shooting flames out in all directions, these natives often have a tendency to spread themselves too thin. Mutable/fire.

♑ **Capricorn** … December 22 – January 20: Key phrase "I use." Capricorns use whatever is available to attain their objectives. These natives concentrate on material goals and are willing to work toward them. Their challenge is to keep a balance between the material and spiritual side of life. Cardinal/earth.

♒ **Aquarius** … January 21 – February 18: Key phrase "I know." Aquarians get sudden flashes of inner knowing unrestricted by established or outworn concepts. Intellectually oriented, they are detached from petty emotions and small thinking. They are humanitarians and strive to make the world a better place. Fixed/air.

♓ **Pisces** … February 19 – March 20: Key phrase "I believe." True freedom for Pisces comes through spiritual orientation. They need time alone to find their own inner guidance to avoid agreeing with others too easily. Their moods are changeable as the moods of the sea. Mutable/water.

TRANSIT: Transits are taken from the ephemeris for the current year of an event. They are then applied by house position and aspect to the natal horoscope to indicate trends and events for that year.

T-SQUARE: A T-Square is a configuration involving three or more planets in square and opposition aspect forming a T. The squares indicate obstacles, challenges and misdirected energy and the opposition calls for a need for balance. Notwithstanding, the T-Square is the most dynamic configuration one can have, especially the Cardinal T-Square. The center planet acts as a piston, giving direction and a central guidance system. Goring has a Cardinal T-Square with Jupiter opposing Saturn and both square the Sun in Capricorn.

29th DEGREE: The 29th degree is more potent than the other degrees for it is a fated degree. It makes destiny and karma more vital. It is fatalistic in that things promised come to fulfillment. Himmler has Venus, Saturn and Neptune in the 29th degree.

WATER SIGNS: Cancer, Scorpio and Pisces. Emotional and sensitive, they desire to protect themselves from others. They are secretive, subtle and indirect. Goebbels has four planets in Scorpio.

WEST: When the majority of planets fall on the right side of the chart (western side), the native's way of life is more dictated by other people. He requires the help of others. Hitler has six planets west, and the Sun, Venus and Mars are in Libra's House that rules other people.

HOROSCOPES

Afra's Horoscope

"I took the tests that unfolded before me as challenges
and emerged with greater inner peace because of them."
Afra

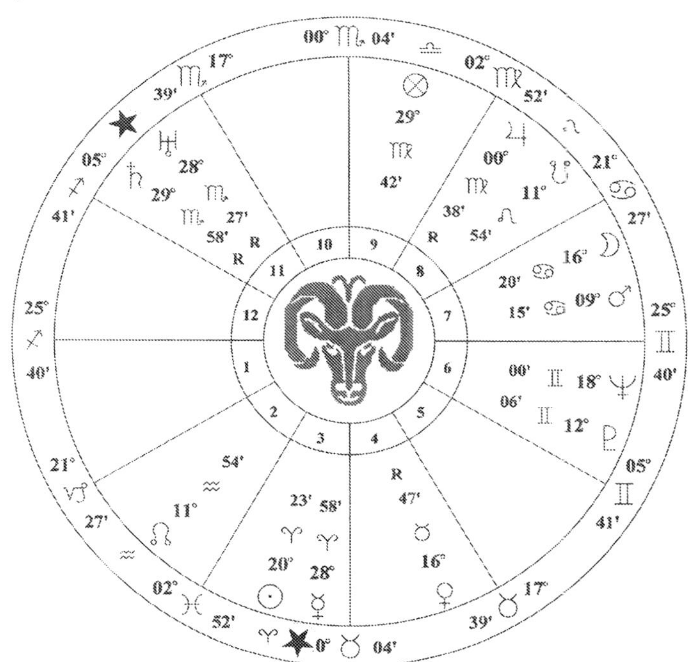

The Sun and Mercury are conjunct in Aries, the first sign in the Zodiac. As such Afra wanted to be first and best in whatever she did. Competitive by nature, she had a strong drive to prove herself.

Like the Ram that symbolizes Aries, she could be impulsive and headstrong. But she was never daunted by obstacles or failure, and much of her strength came from a refusal to admit defeat.

The key phrase for Aries is "I am." Afra wanted to express her individuality – particularly through the spoken and written word as denoted by the Sun and Mercury in the 3rd House. She was adroit in speech and writing.

Her outlook on life is revealed by Sagittarius on the Ascendant. Sagittarius is symbolized by the Centaur, a figure that's half man and half horse. The human half shoots its arrows to the heavens and loves higher knowledge and spiritual philosophy. The horse half is more grounded-- needs challenges and loves to travel to faraway places, mentally and physically.

The Moon and Mars are conjunct in Cancer. An outstanding feature of Afra's Aries Sun Cancer Moon polarity was her uncanny intuitive powers which gain her a reputation as a psychic astrologer.

However, with her home loving Cancer Moon squaring her Aries Sun she was conflicted between a strong family orientation versus her Aries need for independence and to be out in the world where the action is.

When she met Hagan she was carried away with Cancerian fantasies and emotions. That part of her nature was intense, demanding and possessive. When she discovered that Hagan was having an affair she became painfully hurt and resentful.

The Moon in the 7th House depicted her need to feel connected with people. Mars in this house brought her hasty marriage. The afflictions to Mars denoted marital discord and divorce. Like the changing Moon, her feelings about Hagan changed.

The Moon and Mars sextile Venus in the 4th House show that she loved her family and desired domestic harmony. She was a good provider and a wonderful mother.

There are four planets in water signs, the Moon and Mars in Cancer and Saturn and Uranus in Scorpio. Upon meeting Hagan, her emotions blocked out her good judgment indicated by the trines to Jupiter. But as time moved on she felt trapped in their marriage and blamed him. It wasn't easy, but eventually Egon and the study of astrology helped her balance both sides of her nature: the security of homemaking Cancer and the independence of individualistic Aries.

Jupiter, ruler of Sagittarius, is part of a Grand Trine with the Sun, Mercury and Sagittarian Ascendant. Jupiter is retrograde in Virgo indicating that Afra was reserved, unlike typically extroverted Aries and Sagittarius. However, in keeping with Jupiter, she possessed inner optimism.

This Grand Trine is a configuration of honesty and spiritual expansion. With the Sun sextile Neptune and the planets in Cancer, it depicts psychic ability, intelligence and keen powers of observation. Add Venus to this mix and we see that with maturity Afra developed a quality of universal love. She was able to illumine dark places and bring hope and courage to others.

Jupiter in the 8th House was her celestial messenger, her guardian angel ever by her side protecting her.

Afra has a Bucket Chart. The close Saturn/Uranus conjunction makes the handle. These planets in Scorpio gave her powerfully charged emotions, along with a fear of emotional vulnerability. She could be a perfect lover on the physical level, but blocked emotionally. Until she was able to bring her strong desire nature under control she experienced much emotional suffering and pain.

She was determined to dig down to the truths of astrology and life. A gifted psychic, she often gave in-depth metaphysical guidance by briefly glancing at a chart.

Saturn and Uranus are in the 11th House of friends, groups, universal concerns and wishes. While Afra was ambitious, her heart's desire is to help humanity. Over time she grew into a broader understanding and an inner awareness of the higher purposes of life.

Jupiter squares Saturn and Uranus. At times Afra was held down by financial or other problems that limited her freedom to act and expand.

Venus in Taurus denotes a strong love nature. Venus in the 4th House shows there was lovingness at the roots of her being. However, Venus retrograde indicates it was difficult for her to express love freely. The end of her life was pleasant and peaceful.

Afra has several fixed stars. Unlike the malefic stars shown in many of the Nazi charts, hers are benefic. The Sun conjunct Baten Kaitos denotes a philosophical interpretation of events. Mercury conjunct Mirach signifies sympathy, understanding and a desire to help the world. Saturn conjunct Bungula shows occult leanings.

She was an old soul whose mission is to inspire and teach others.

Adolph Hitler's Horoscope

"The man who is born to be a dictator is not compelled, he wills."

Adolph Hitler

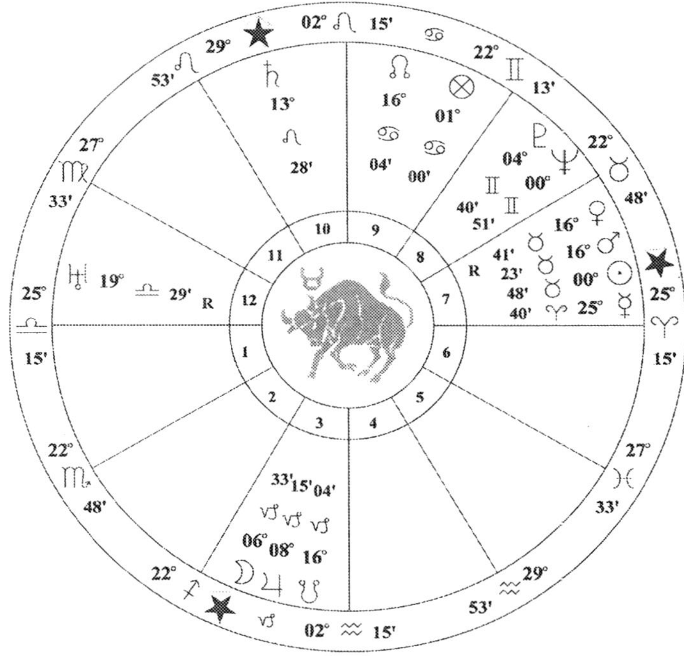

The fixed signs manifest as "Will," and Hitler has four planets in fixed signs: the Sun, Venus and Mars in Taurus and Saturn in Leo. The positive attributes of fixity are constancy and reliability. However, the fixed emphasis in Hitler's horoscope together with

Venus and Mars squaring Saturn denote extreme stubbornness and self-will. Once he made up his mind about anything, he absolutely refused to change regardless of the consequences. Saturn afflicted in the 10th House of career designates his megalomaniac determination to acquire power and control by the force of his will.

His fixed squares indicate deeply ingrained patterns of behavior, signifying harsh lessons he failed to learn over many lifetimes. He refused to change himself in any way whatsoever. As far back as he could remember his relationship with his father was nothing but brutal beatings and a battle of wills. Being powerless under his father's domination from an early age, control became a major issue in his life. He also suffered frustration trying to live up to his mother's strict definition of propriety.

Leo rules the heart. But with Venus and Mars squaring Saturn in Leo, he was a cold-hearted man. He always felt unloved, wrong and inferior.

His Saturn squares also indicate sexual inhibitions. To compensate for his sexual inadequacy he strove to dominate and control every area of Geli's life. But he was a cold man, and his affair with her was mostly based on sex. Unable to fill the emptiness and lack of love within, he wanted everyone to love him.

His sexuality was compulsive and far from normal as shown by Mars conjunct Venus retrograde and both square Saturn in Leo, Venus and Mars inconjunct Uranus, the Moon inconjunct Pluto, and the Moon conjunct the fixed star Facies.

The inconjunct aspect is 150 degrees apart, that is, 30 degrees less than a 180 degree opposition. Unlike an opposition that leads one directly to their objective, it's necessary to take an indirect path. The three inconjuncts in Hitler's horoscope show he had to take perverted ways to achieve sexual satisfaction. The Moon inconjunct Pluto indicates one partner or the other exerting sadistic control. Sadomasochism expresses sexually as weakness and submission and is indicated astrologically by feminine signs – in Hitler's case the five planets in Taurus and Capricorn. Taurus is the sign that wants love, sexual outlet and the security of possessions. Hitler made up for his repressed sexuality and inability to love by an overwhelming need to own the world.

Mars is the planet of action; Saturn restrains and holds back. Hitler alternated between dynamic oratory and apathy, aggressive action and much time sleeping, short working hours and outright laziness. One tendency of Taureans is to lazily enjoy the good life.

The fixed squares also show Hitler's opinions concerning politics were dogmatic and intolerant. All alternative ideas were violently rejected; nobody was ever allowed to criticize his assumptions.

Hitler has five planets in Earth Signs: the Sun, Venus and Mars in Taurus and the Moon and Jupiter in Capricorn. Earth Signs are materialistic. As a Taurean he loved ownership and had a natural ability to accumulate money and material resources. The Moon and Jupiter conjunct in Capricorn denote organizational and administrative ability.

He has no planets in water that normally signifies personal warmth and sympathy. He compensated for a lack of feeling and lovingness through attainment of power, money, possessions and land, as shown by his five planets in earth signs.

The Sun, Venus, Mars and Mercury reside in the 7th House ruling other people and open enemies. Hitler surrounded himself Nazi adherents whom he depended on at all times. However, his incessant drive for absolute power made it difficult for his associates to cope with his manic demands. Ultimately, this caused alienation and made open enemies of countless people throughout the world.

With the Moon and Jupiter conjunct in Capricorn in the 3rd House of communication and trining the Sun, Venus and Mars, he shrewdly tuned into the minds and emotions of his audiences to gain their confidence and cooperation. The compelling emotional bond he created with audiences of thousands gave him an outlet for his repressed sexuality. This left him perspiring and drained, a satiated lover.

Venus and Jupiter are benefic planets. He was lucky, and more than a few times he barely escaped with his life.

The Moon trining the Sun signify Hitler's conscious will (the Sun) and his subconscious (the Moon) were in harmony. He had administrative capacity to recruit the right person with the right abilities to accomplish his ends. He was capable of great determination and perseverance when it came to manipulating people and acquiring power and possessions.

As mentioned, the Moon and Jupiter are in Capricorn. Although the favorable trines brought him high position and great material benefits, the Moon's warm nurturing qualities and Jupiter's natural optimism are replaced with Capricorn's drive for power and status.

Neptune and Pluto, two undercover planets, are conjunct in the 8th House of death and other planes of being. The Moon inconjuncts Pluto, ruler of demons. The Satanic ritual Hitler experienced to gain control of powerful occult forces back-fired when the demon seduced him with lies and promises. And Hitler was not above seizing any advantage with lies, treachery, unscrupulousness and murder.

Neptune and Pluto sextiling the MC show that he grasped as no one before him what he could accomplish with a combination of propaganda and terrorism. Through newspapers, radio and loudspeaker, he was able to manipulate, control and then deprive eighty million people of independent thought. However, the Saturn squares brought his inevitable downfall.

Uranus conjunct his Libra Ascendant explains the charismatic magnetism that drew other people to him. He had an inventive approach. With Saturn sextiling Uranus he periodically came up with unusual but effective ideas. On the other hand, Mercury opposes Uranus, denoting a tendency to impulsively jump into radical projects. Most people were unaware of his astrological occult interests because Uranus is in the 12th House of secrets.

Mercury in Aries indicates Hitler was mentally sharp and quick. Put him in the spotlight and he was a dynamic, fiery speaker. Mercury opposing Uranus and the Ascendant signify he was also a demagogue, arrogantly demanding that everyone follow his ideas. He had to lead; he felt everyone should bow before his superior intelligence. But Mercury is in the 7th House brought sudden upsets and estrangements with others, especially his fellow Nazis.

That Hitler became insane is indicated by Mercury opposing Uranus and the Moon in the 3rd House inconjunct Pluto.

Geli Raubal's Horoscope

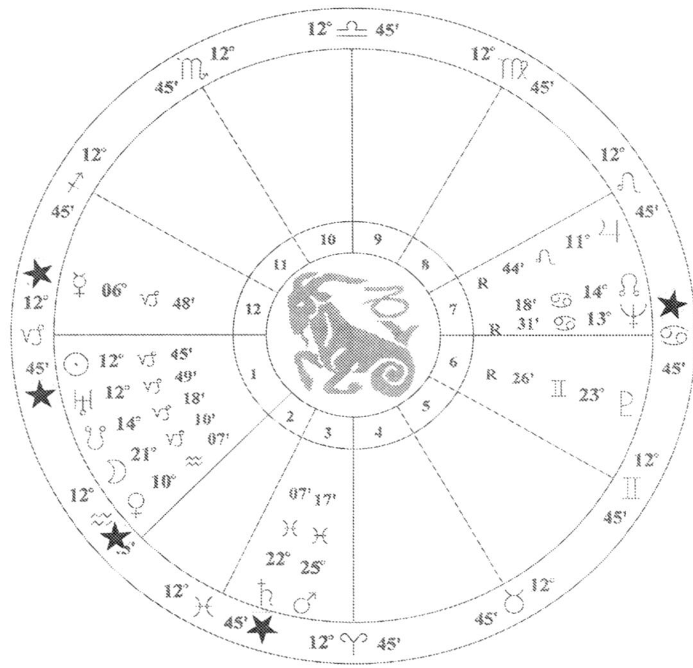

Perhaps most important for our purposes, Geli Raubal has Facies, the fixed star connected with suicide and murder, conjunct a planet, as does Hitler and Eva Braun. In Geli's case, Facies conjuncts Mercury. Her death was reported to be a suicide, but reliable sources claimed it wasn't.

The Sun and Uranus conjunct the fixed star Manubrium. This star is often found in charts indicating an unusual sex life. Much materialism and temptings of pleasure and self-indulgence.

Markab conjuncts Saturn denoting a violent death.

In Geli's flat chart Mercury, the Sun, Uranus, South Node and Moon are in Capricorn. Capricorn is an earth sign, and Geli was self-centered, shrewd, money-minded and ambitious. She had a materialistic outlook concerning relationships. The Sun and Mercury conjunct Uranus signify personal magnetism that made her attractive to males. But she was independent and could be contrary and willful.

Mercury, Sun and Uranus oppose Neptune. Her overly vivid imagination wasn't always reliable. She was deceptive, and she was deceived by others. Emotional chaos.

Venus in Aquarius indicates an unconventional love nature.

Mars conjuncts Saturn in Pisces and squares Pluto. She had sadistic tendencies together with periods of great jealousy, and she could easily loose her temper. Sometimes these squares indicate a violent death. The conjunction implies laziness.

The Moon sextiles Mars and Saturn. Good ties with mother. Responsible.

Geli's Sun and Uranus trine Hitler's Venus and Mars and conjunct his Jupiter and Moon. Theirs was an exciting and powerfully magnetic attraction. Hitler was infatuated with his niece, but her unpredictability irritated him. Still, there was a protective urge and benevolence.

Geli's Moon squares Hitler's Uranus and opposes his Mercury, arousing different viewpoints and annoyance. Hitler was unpredictable and inconsiderate, often disregarding Geli. The attraction between them was unconventional.

Geli's badly afflicted Neptune opposes Hitler's Jupiter and Moon. She was strongly tempted to cheat or deceive him. He found her elusive and hard to pin down; he never felt he could trust her.

Hitler's afflicted Saturn squares Geli's Jupiter and opposes her Venus. He was extremely possessive, jealous and demanding. He continually put obstacles in the path of her ambitions to be a singer so she felt confined and frustrated. As far as she was concerned he was unjust, selfish and demanding.

Eva Braun's Horoscope

EVA BRAUN
Tuesday, February 06, 1912 5:30:00 AM
Munich, Germany
Time Zone: -01:00 (CET)
Longitude: 011° E 34'
Latitude: 48° N 08'
Koch Houses
Tropical Zodiac
Mean Nodes
Night Chart

Astrology Services Courtesy of:
Roberleigh H Claigh

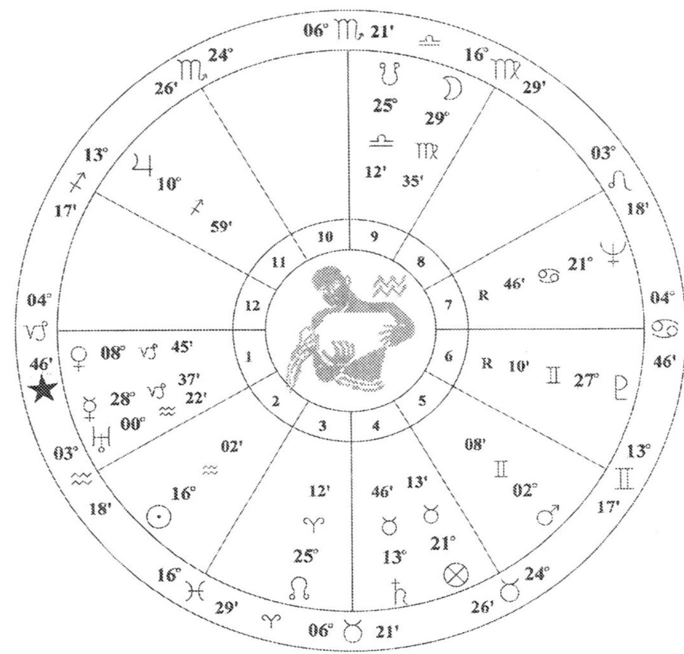

She has Venus conjunct the fixed star Facies, denoting her suicide. Still, she has three favorable fixed stars: Pluto conjuncts Betelguese, Saturn conjuncts Almach, and Uranus conjuncts Albireo. In many ways she was content being Hitler's mistress.

She was born under Aquarius, the sign of friendship.

Venus is in Capricorn and trines Saturn. Those whom she befriended had her unswerving loyalty. She had a way of growing on people.

The Sun squares Saturn in Taurus depicting disappointments and frustrations because in past lifetimes she frustrated and disappointed others.

Eva's Venus conjuncts Hitler's Moon and Jupiter and makes wide trines to Hitler's Sun, Venus and Mars denoting loyalty, love and affection. However, keep in mind that Hitler had little capacity for love. Eva had a soothing, calming effect on him.

On the other side of the coin, Eva's Saturn and Hitler's Saturn are conjunct. And Eva's Saturn squares his Venus and Mars. Not exactly a love aspect, and there wasn't much sexual activity going either. In the bedroom Hitler was Eva's groveling slave. Otherwise, she quietly suffered his tyranny.

Hermann Goring's Horoscope

"Every time I face Hitler, my heart falls into my pants."
Goring

After retirement, Hermann Goring's father had little money apart from his state pension to support his wife Franziska and their five children. Herr Epenstein, a wealthy Jewish bachelor and godfather to the Goring children, invited the struggling family to live in his castle. During this time still a comparatively young woman, Franziska became Epenstein's lover. While Franziska entertained Herr Epenstein upstairs in the master bedroom, her aging husband and children were quartered downstairs.

In Hermann's horoscope, the Sun and Mercury are in Capricorn, the Moon and Uranus are conjunct in Scorpio, and Scorpio is on the Ascendant. The Capricorn/Scorpio combination showed he was shrewd even as a child. He knew what was going on upstairs.

His father indulged his whims, as shown by the Sun squaring easy-going indulgent Jupiter. He told his son, "You can do anything, as long as you do it with a smile."

In strong contrast, the Sun and Mercury squaring stern Saturn describes Hermann's other father figure, Epenstein. Epenstein was not above using physical force to teach discipline and accomplishment to the headstrong boy. He demanded a lot from Hermann and his brothers and sisters in return for allowing the Goring family to live in his house.

Hermann consequently developed an inferiority complex. He was never able to stand up to powerful authority figures such as Epenstein and later on, Hitler.

However, the T-Square with the Sun, Mars and Jupiter, and Saturn indicates that at an early age he developed a seesaw pattern of hard work and indulgence. He overloaded himself with responsibilities to prove his self-worth (Saturn), and then compensated with all kinds of hedonistic pleasures (Jupiter). It's likely he became impotent as a result of the drugs he took after he was wounded in Hitler's Putsch.

He had a keen interest in history as shown by the Sun and Mercury in Capricorn. Epenstein's castle gave him a view of medieval grandeur and awoke a desire for feudal power he never lost. He loved playing the knight in shining armor, the crusading and triumphant hero. He had a strong tendency toward acts of physical prowess and courage as denoted by Mars and Jupiter conjunct in Aries.

The Moon conjunct Uranus and Mars inconjunct Uranus indicate he was rebellious with no respect for authority unless it was powerful enough to keep him in line. When boarding school proved to be a disaster his father enrolled him in a military school. He immediately took to military life.

Goring's Capricorn Sun/Scorpio Moon combination imparted excellent qualities for a military career: discipline, courage and strategic ability. This powerful polarity is also good for government posts, police and investigative work. On the down side, he was ruthless in pursuit of personal ambition, and always had some scheme to use other people for his own purposes.

Goring was highly intelligent as indicated by Uranus in Scorpio ruling the 3rd House and conjunct the Moon and quintile the Sun. He possessed a sharp, detective-like mind that quickly exposed the core of any situation. He instinctively saw through falsity and disguise. He knew how to dig the truth out of others, but was secretive, devious and evasive himself

The powerful Scorpio influence in his horoscope made him suspicious of everyone. As Hitler's second man, he constantly schemed and manipulated from behind the scenes. He harbored grudges but never allowed his face to show them. He brutally eliminated anyone who stood in his way. However, when it was to his advantage, he could be infinitely cautious as shown by Saturn trine Neptune and Pluto. He was a man of no morals.

Mercury conjuncts Venus in Sagittarius and Venus trines Jupiter. People were generally oblivious to his sinister qualities and saw him only as outgoing and expansive with a powerful magnetism. He had a genial personality and sense of humor that he exploited for ulterior motives.

As shown by his 2nd House Sun making the T-Square with Jupiter and Saturn he was a greedy man. He helped those who helped him and destroyed those in his way. He became one of the richest men in Germany, but left his debts largely unpaid, assuming he could get away with it.

This is a Bucket Chart. Eight planets are located on one half of the wheel, while a "handle" is formed by Neptune and Pluto closely conjunct in Gemini in the 7th House of other people. Neptune and Pluto are a channel for all the energy expressed by the bucket planets and the means by which Goring went after what he wanted. He was never honest about his motives: he always kept something hidden from others. He secretly plotted to gain total control over those weaker than himself.

The Sun square Jupiter denotes show, ostentation and over-indulgence and his Scorpio Moon and Ascendant indicate an all or nothing path. He loved to eat and his weight rose to 264 pounds on a 5'10" frame. He was an exhibitionist who paraded around in dress uniforms, gold braid, medals and decorations and showed off his possessions.

In 1923, his doctors prescribed morphine for pain caused by poisoned wounds received during Hitler's unsuccessful Putsch. Two years later he was showing the worst symptoms of morphine addiction and was periodically treated to remove the toxins from his system. By the early part of the World War II, he had deteriorated under his addiction and was beset with doubts, depression and fear. He spent more and more time at his huge forest estate.

Mercury conjuncts the fixed star Polis depicting a propensity for power and prosperity. Saturn conjuncting the fixed star Algorab gave him logic, executive ability, and a keen analysis of prevailing economic conditions. It envisaged great ambition and brought him outstanding success, but Algorab (sometimes referred to as The Buzzard) also heralded Goring's gross materialism, violence and destruction.

At the Nuremberg Trials in 1946, he was sentenced to death by hanging, but to avoid the humiliation he took his own life with poison.

Rudolph Hess's Horoscope

"Do not seek Adolph Hitler with your brains; all of you will find him with the strength of your hearts."

Rudolph Hess

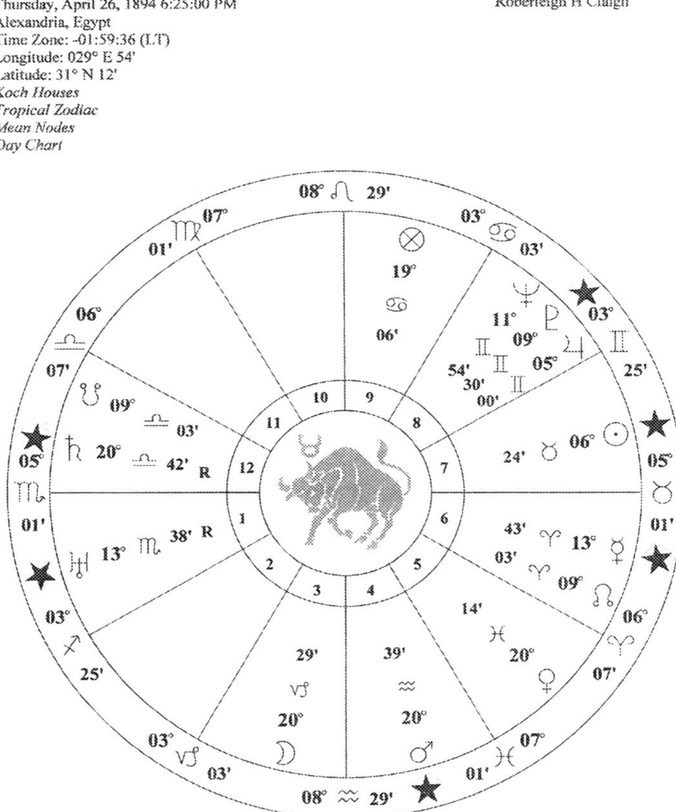

Perhaps the first thing that attracts the eye in this horoscope is the Sun in Taurus conjuncting the fixed star Hamal, often referred to by astrologers as "the dive into the abyss". Hamal also denotes violence, cruelty, premeditated crime and evil associates.

There are some interesting similarities between Hess's horoscope and Hitler's.

1.   They both have the Sun in earthy materialistic Taurus.

2.   They both have the Moon in detriment in Capricorn. This unhappy placement signifies they were basically cold and distant, unable to express the tender, emotional side of the Moon. Subconscious feelings of inferiority impelled them to prove themselves in a drive for prestige and power. Ever reaching for the mountaintops, they viewed others only as useful stepping-stones.

3.   They have Mercury in Aries depicting a tendency to see things from an excessively personal and narcissistic point of view.

4.   There are several similar house positions. They both have the Sun in the 7th House showing a need for the assistance and cooperation of other people. They have the Moon in the 3rd House, signifying their thinking was subconsciously affected by childhood programming. Mercury afflicted in Aries indicates that wrong thinking habits caused illness affecting their brains. Neptune and Pluto conjunct in the 8th House denote a fascination with death and life after death.

5.   Uranus conjunct the Ascendant shows involvement in revolutionary activities and social philosophies, and they believed in astrology and the occult.

However, there are some important differences. Whereas Hitler's mother was not a demonstrative person, Hess's mother was downright cold as seen by the T-Square between his Capricorn Moon, Saturn and Mercury. It's likely his mother never gave him a word of love or encouragement. He had a depressing childhood. Consequently, functioning in the adult world was extremely difficult for him.

Hitler's Moon, on the other hand, conjuncts Jupiter in the 3rd House and makes favorable trines with the Sun, Venus and Mars. This gave Hitler a good deal of confidence in matters of communication.

Hitler has sociable Libra on the Ascendant, while Hess has introverted Scorpio in that position. Hitler's Saturn is in the authoritative sign of Leo and placed at the top of his chart on the powerful though malevolent fixed star Acubens. Hess's Saturn is retrograde in Libra in the hidden 12th House denoting that despite his ambitions, he was more comfortable behind the scenes and went through all kinds of torment when he had to speak in public.

Hess's Grand Trine with Saturn, Neptune and Mars in the 4th House indicates his parents had ambitious dreams for him to succeed and they constantly pushed him to work harder. But with Mars square Uranus, he never knew when he might displease his father, causing him to blow up in a fit of anger or give him a beating. Afraid of upsetting his parents, he harbored all his frustrations, anger and resentment inside himself. These feelings would build up over a long period of time, ultimately breaking out in outbursts of brutal aggression.

Having so many traits in common, it's not surprising that Hess and Hitler developed a fairly close relationship. That is, as close as Hitler was capable with anyone. Hess was one of the few people that Hitler referred to with the familiar du.

When Hitler came into power he appointed Hess Deputy Fuhrer because he could depend on his unconditional loyalty and compliance. Yet Hess's sense of inadequacy led him to be progressively excluded from policy making. Eventually, he acted partly as Hitler's secretary and partly as a deputy in minor state affairs. Yet he was always waiting "for the Fuhrer to recognize his reticence" and give it priority.

Mercury badly aspected in Hess's 6th House makes it clear he had all kinds of fears and worries about his work and his health. He constantly suffered from physical complaints largely psychological in origin. However, Uranus Rising in Scorpio and making a Yode with Mercury and Neptune indicate that unorthodox sex habits and guilt thereof resulted in inner tension. For years he went from doctor to doctor. Finally he lost confidence in the entire medical profession and resorted to nature healers, mesmerists and astrologers.

To some Hess was known as "Fraulein Anna." Homosexuality is disclosed in his chart by Venus square Neptune in the 8th House of Sex and the T-Square between the Moon in Capricorn, Mercury and Saturn that show he didn't like women very much. Nevertheless, on Hitler's suggestion, he married. His wife complained, "I have as much experience out of our marriage as a candidate for confirmation." Despite their limited sex life they longed for the all-important male child. They consulted astrologers and magicians and finally, a son was born.

The aforementioned Yode and the Moon sextiling Uranus in the 1st House indicate his strong interest in occultism and spirit phenomena ranging from the less reputable to the scientific such as astrology. He made a study of the efforts of practitioners of terrestrial radiation, animal magnetism, the pendulum and ways of foretelling the future. He eventually established the Rudolph Hess Hospital for the sole purpose of testing cures that weren't recognized by the medical profession.

At the time of his sudden and ill-conceived flight transiting Saturn was passing through the 7th House and opposed natal Uranus, setting off his Mars/Uranus square. His life was changed forever.

Heinrich Himmler's Horoscope

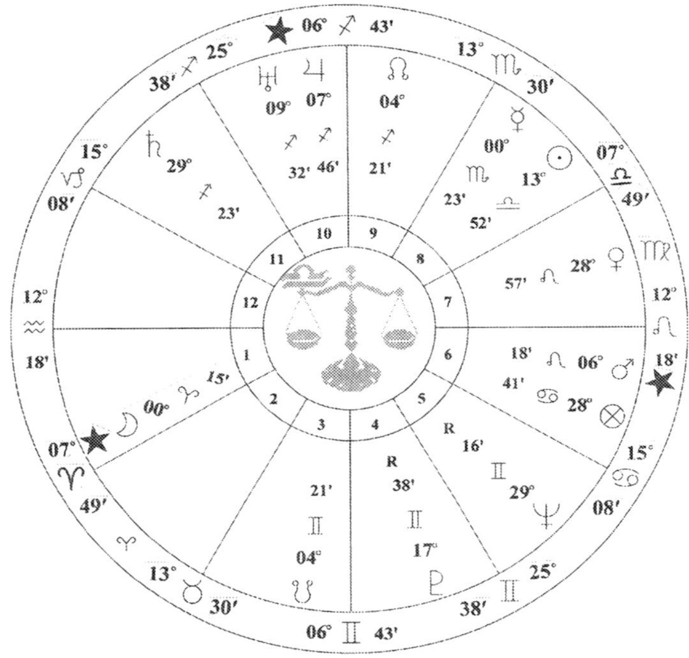

It's been claimed that Himmler had no real ego so he wasn't aware a Doppelganger was working through him. A Doppelganger is said to be a person's ghostly double bent on terror and inquisition. Well, I thought, how could someone have no real ego? But his horoscope seems to bear this out. With the Sun in detriment in Libra his ego had to step aside for others. He was terrified of the other Party leaders and made all kinds of concessions to keep the peace. In no important matter did he ever contradict Hitler, and he would go to any length to appease him and to prevent his rages.

In this respect, it's hard to understand how Himmler ever managed to become one of the most powerful men in Germany, controlling both the SS and the Gestapo. First, Hitler had an uncanny way of seeing behind a person's outer personality. There was something about Himmler that gave him the impression he had strong leadership and organizational ability, firm determination, and a capacity to handle overwhelmingly tough and dangerous situations.

These characteristics are also revealed in Himmler's horoscope. The Sun trines Pluto, and while Pluto is the smallest planet, it's ten times more powerful for better or worse than Mars. Himmler possessed intense concentration, willpower, determination and ability to take control. He knew from his gut exactly what was going on and how to act with the most efficient use of energy and resources.

The Sun is in the 8th House that's always been associated with death and destruction. As founder and officer-in-charge of the Nazi concentration camps and death squads, Himmler had final command and responsibility for the concentration camps and people considered to be a threat to Hitler's regime.

He also has a Grand Trine with the Moon, Mars, Jupiter and Uranus. Jupiter and Uranus conjunct in the 10th House signify that he was an ambitious social reformer and especially lucky career-wise. He frequently used original methods to get the job done. A part of him was concerned with the moral consequences of his actions which brought him painful inner conflict resulting from Hitler's manic demands.

Yet, as indicated by the T-square with the Moon, Saturn and Neptune, he was not above using secret and underhanded means to achieve his own ends. Terribly insecure, he always had to prove himself.

Prone to colds, lung infections and excruciating stomach pains, he periodically retreated from reality to his bed. He alternated between self-pity and resentment.

Saturn afflicted in Sagittarius shows that he was intolerant of his childhood religious beliefs. He turned away from the Catholic Church and became much involved with astrology and the occult. However, with Neptune part of the T-Square he was full of crackpot ideas. He was obsessed with developing a master race of "sacred" German blood. To this end, a chain of maternity homes were set up, and all married or single woman were encouraged to produce children as their "sacred duty" to the Fuhrer and the German race. "Racially valuable" young women were urged to mate with SS men with an "Aryan" pedigree. Single women were not required to get married; the children of such unions were considered legitimate.

With Jupiter and Uranus opposing Pluto in the 4th House he lived in the midst of drastic changes – war, revolution and violence.

Obsessed with fanatic occult opinions, he set up a school of occultism and ordered many high-rank SS and Gestapo men to take courses in meditation, transcendentalism and magic. He also had a select few perform satanic practices, supposedly to transform them into supermen. He was a believer in the superiority of the Aryan race, and as head of the SS he was in charge of killing hundreds of thousands of people that threatened the Nazis, the Jews and other so-called inferior races.

Still, his Grand Trine involving the Jupiter Uranus conjunction signifies that he had some understanding of astrology and the occult. He began important projects at certain phases of the Moon, similar to his ancestors who planted crops according to the Moon. He coerced astrologer Wilhelm Wulff to do personal readings for him, as well as horoscopes on Hitler, Churchill, the King of England and Stalin.

There are no planets in Earth. His feet weren't on the ground. His ambitions were unrealistic.

Although Venus conjunct the fixed start Regulus brought him authority and command, the harsh squares and opposition aspects together with the following malefic fixed stars took precedence in his horoscope. Jupiter and Uranus conjunct the rapacious star

Antares. Mars conjunct North Ascelli introduced an element of under-handedness and premeditated evil. The Moon conjunct Difda foretold his inhibitions, ill health, misfortune and final self-destruction.

After Germany lost the war Himmler was captured by the British Army. He bit into a cyanide capsule that was inserted in a tooth and swallowed the poison. Minutes later he was dead.

Ernst Rohm's Horoscope

"Since I am an immature and wicked person war and unrest appeal to me more than well balanced bourgeois order."

Ernst Rohm

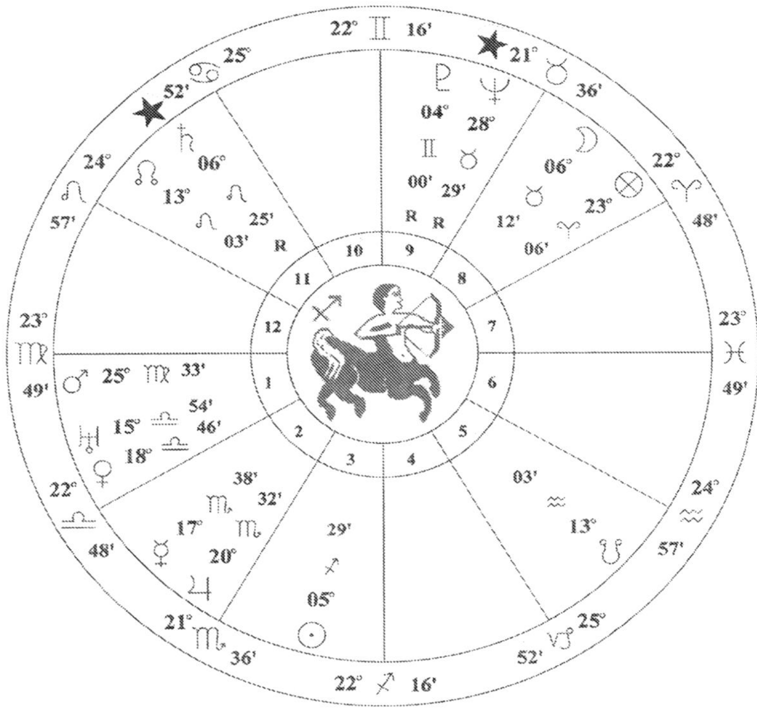

Rohm has the Sun in Sagittarius and the Moon and Neptune widely conjunct in Taurus. Taurus adds stability, determination and fixity of purpose to a Sagittarius tendency to fly off in many different directions. Thus, there is increased potential for professional and material success. However, due to the negative influences in Rohm's horoscope, this polarity gave him an irresolute, pleasure-oriented nature, with the id gaining the upper hand over the ego.

On the plus side, the Sun trining Saturn denotes excellent organizational ability. He helped organize the first Nazi strong arm squads that developed into the SA, the army of storm troopers he commanded.

Rohm was a skillful military commander and fighter as signified by Mercury and Jupiter sextile the Mars/Ascendant conjunction. Strong and muscular, he loved strenuous physical exercise and projected himself forcefully.

As a Sagittarius/Taurus person, he was chunky and bull-necked with a reddish complexion. A native of Sagittarius, Rohm was an adventurous gambler ready to try his luck at anything new.

Oppositions in charts work through other people. Altogether, there are four opposition aspects in Rohm's horoscope. The Sun in the 3rd House of communication and thoughts opposes Pluto and Neptune in the 9th House. Mercury and Jupiter are conjunct in Scorpio and oppose Neptune. He was secretive and devious, sharper than a two-edged sword. These oppositions also caused distortions and confused thinking and corrupted Rohm's morals and ethics. Bad karma, deception from others and unrealistic optimism created blind spots and bad judgment.

Rohm wanted to transform the world according to his needs, and he alienated others by trying to shove his opinions down their throats. He had no principles and no conscience regarding violence and murder, and he was involved with people who were similarly confused, manipulative, tyrannical and brutal.

Furthermore, these oppositions indicate he would swing back and forth from one extreme to the other. In his work, he was disciplined, regimented, organized and exacting, but in his private life he was driven to a wanton pursuit of pleasure, sex and debauchery.

Rohm was a homosexual as indicated by Mercury and Jupiter in Scorpio opposing Neptune, and by Venus and Uranus conjunct. Typical of outspoken Sagittarius, he flaunted his homosexuality.

With Saturn conjunct the fixed star North Ascelli the road to fame beckoned Rohm. Neptune conjunct the fixed star Alcyone denotes his bold military career and secrecy. Both fixed stars foretold a violent death when he made the fatal mistake of trying to force his ideas on Hitler, who never conceded to anyone.

Albert Speer's Horoscope

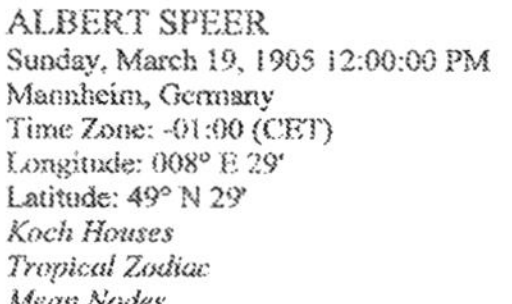

ALBERT SPEER
Sunday, March 19, 1905 12:00:00 PM
Mannheim, Germany
Time Zone: -01:00 (CET)
Longitude: 008° E 29'
Latitude: 49° N 29'
Koch Houses
Tropical Zodiac
Mean Nodes
Day Chart

Astrology Services Courtesy of:
Roberleigh H Claigh

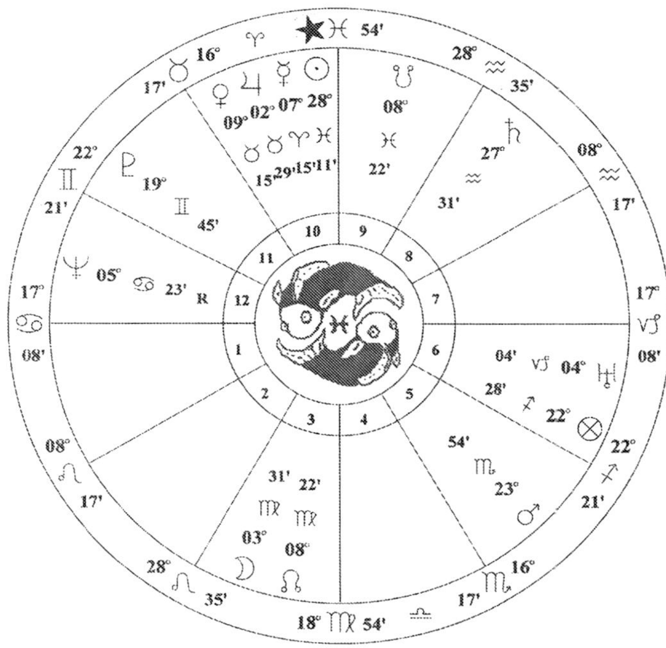

Speer was a native of Pisces, the sign symbolized by two fish tied together with a ribbon. One fish is struggling to swim upstream while the other fish floats downstream with the current. This symbol demonstrates that Pisces is a dual sign. One side can be highly spiritual, while the other side may passively float along with the group. Pisceans can get into a lot of trouble if they get in with a bad crowd.

With the Sun in Pisces and the Ascendant and Neptune conjunct in Cancer, all water signs, Speer was emotional, sensitive, changeable and imaginative.

The Sun and Mercury are located in the 10th House of profession and standing in the world. Speer worked hard to acquire the necessary knowledge and skills to attain his ambitions. He had strong organizational ability.

The Sun and Mercury are part of a T-Square with Uranus and Neptune. This is an important configuration because Neptune, the planet of illusion, is Pisces' ruler. Although the Moon in Virgo would ordinarily denote keen judgment, with Neptune's involvement in this T-Square Speer seldom saw things clearly or realistically. Hitler's emotionally rousing speeches, grandiose schemes and double talk blinded him to his innate Piscean intuition. Like so many others, he glossed over discrepancies concerning Hitler and the Nazi Party, assuming they would be straightened out in time. He was not above scheming to achieve his ambitions. With Neptune in the 12th House, there are secrets and mysteries concerning Speer we will never know.

Uranus, as part in this T-Square, shows that Speer was a misguided revolutionary. Yet his architecture was conventional for he undeviatingly followed Hitler's demands and he, too, was reluctant to completely let go of the past.

The Sun conjuncts Scheat, one of the most famous fixed stars. As part of the T-Square, Scheat brought out the lowest side of Speer's nature and led him into calamity and ultimate downfall.

Pluto squares the Sun and MC. Obsessively ambitious, he readily went along with Hitler's wild pursuit of power. Pluto is the most destructive of all the planets, and here we see treachery, deception and destruction on all levels – coming from secret enemies, as well as with his own self-destruction and failure while bringing many others down with him.

As with Hitler, Speer has Mars squares Saturn. However, Hitler's Saturn is in detriment in control hungry Leo and Mars is detriment in lazy Taurus. Speer's Mars is at home in Scorpio indicating self-discipline, and Saturn is at home in group minded

Aquarius. They both were ambitious, but Speer was more disciplined and better able to sublimate his will to work with others for a common cause.

There are some excellent aspects in Speer's chart. The Sun trining Mars in Scorpio gave him great energy, a strong will to succeed and assured professional success.

The Moon in Virgo is a stabilizing and energizing influence. This Virgo part of his nature was sharp of mind, exacting, hard working and got the job done – quite different from his dreamy imaginative Piscean side. But his desire for perfectionism in his work made him blind to larger issues. Pisces is the most dual of the dual mutable signs.

The Grand Trine with the Moon, Venus and Jupiter conjunct, and Uranus was very lucky, especially career-wise. The Venus Jupiter conjunction in Taurus signifies he was indeed a gifted architect. Uranus in Capricorn shows that he made important changes in Hitler's huge power structures.

Nevertheless, looking at this horoscope as a whole, it's clear the destructive side outweighs the positive. While he may have appeared to be a rather pleasant, unthreatening person, in essence he was as scheming, unscrupulous and power hungry as the rest of the Nazi leaders.

BIBLIOGRAPHY

Bullock, Alan. *Hitler A Study In Tyranny*, Harper & Row Publishers, NY, 1962

Chambertin, Ilya. *Astro-Analysis*, Lancer Books, NY, 1970

Cornell, H. L., M.D. *Encyclopedia of Medical Astrology*, Los Angeles, CA, 1933

Dolan, Edward, Jr. *Adolph Hitler A Portrait in Tyranny,* Dodd, Mead & Company, NY, 1980

Editors of Time-Life Books. *The Center of the Web*, Alexandria, VA, 1990 Alexandria, VA, 1992

Elson, Robert & Editors. *Prelude To War*, Time-Life Books, NY, 1976

Editors of Time-Life Books. *Descent Into Nightmare,*

Engelmann, Bernt. *Hitler's Germany,* Pantheon Books, NY, 1986

Erickson, John. *The Road To Berlin*, Westview Press, Boulder, CO, 1983

Erlewine, Stephen, compiler. *The Circle Book of Charts*, Circle Books, Ann Arbor, MI 1972

Fuchs, Thomas. *A Concise Biography of Adolph Hitler.* Berkley Books, NY, 2000

Flood, Charles. *Hitler, the Path to Power*, Houghton Mifflin Company, Boston, MA, 1989

Greene, Liz. *Saturn, A New Look at an Old Devil*, Samuel Weiser Inc. York Beach, Maine, 1976

Haffner, Sebastain. *Defying Hitler*, Picador, US, 2003

Hall, Manly. *The Secret Teachings Of All Ages*, Philosophical Research Society, Los Angeles, 1975

Heck, Alphons. *A Child of Hitler*, Renaissance House Publishers, Phoenix, AZ, 1988

Heiber, Helmut. *Goebbels*, Hawthorne Books, NY, 1972

Herzstein, Robert. *The Nazis*, Time-Life Books, Alexandria, VA, 1980

Hickey, Isabel. *Astrology, A Cosmic Science*, CRCS Publications, Sebastopol, CA, 1992

Hodgson, Joan. *Astrology The Sacred Science.* The White Eagle Publishing Trust, England, 1978

Howe, Ellic. *Astrology, Its Role in World War II*, Walker & Company, NY

Isherwood, Christopher. *The Berlin Stories*, New Directions Publishing, NY, 1945

Irving, David. *Goring, a Biography*, Morrow Publishers, NY, 1989

Irving, David. *Hitler's War*, The Viking Press, NY, 1977

Kelly, C. Brian. *Best Little Stories From World War II*, Cumberland House Publishing, Nashville, TN, 1989

Langer, Walter. *The Mind of Adolph Hitler*, Basic Books Inc. NY, 1972

Levenda, Peter. *Unholy Alliance, A History of Nazi Involvement with the Occult*, Continuum International Publishing Group, NY, 2005

Manvell, Roger. *Goring*, Simon & Shuster, 1962

Marion March & Joan McEvers. *The Only Way To Learn Astrology, volume1*, Astro-Analysis Publications, San Diego, CA, 1981

Moody, Raymond A. *Life After Life,* Guideposts, Carmel, CA, 1975

Nebenzal, Harold. *Café Berlin*, The Overlook Press, Woodstock, NY, 1992

Owings, Alison. *Frauen, German Women Recall the Third Reich*, Rangers University Press, New Brunswick, NJ, 1992

Payne, Robert. *The Life and Death of Adolph Hitler*, Praege Publisher, NY, 1973

Ravenscroft, Trevor. *The Spear of Destiny*, Red Wheel/Weiser LLC, Boston, 1982

Reiss, Curt. *Joseph Goebbels, A Biography*, Doubleday, 1948

Richardson, Horst Fuchs Richardson (Editor). *Seig Heil! War Letters of A Tank Gunner*, Achon Books, Hamden, CT, 1987

Ross, Stewart. *Causes & Consequences of World War II*, Steck-Vaughn Publishers, Austin, TX, 1996

Samuel, Wolfgang. *German Boy*, Broadway Books, NY, 2000

Sevareid, Eric. *WWII*, Prentice Hall Press, NY, 1989

Sakoian & Acker. *The Astrologer's Handbook*. Harper Perenial, NY, 1987

Shirer, William. *Berlin Diary*, Alfred A. Knoff Publisher, NY, 1941

Shirer, William. *End of a Berlin Diary*, Alfred A. Knoff Publisher, NY, 1947

Shirer, William. *The Rise and Fall of The Third Reich*, Simon & Shuster, NY, 1960

Shirer, William. *The Nightmare Years*, Little, Brown & Company, Boston, 1984

Sklar, D. *The Nazis and The Occult*. Dorset Press, New York, 1989

Smith, Bradley. *Heinrich Himmler, a Nazi In The Making*

Smith, Howard. *Last Train From Berlin*, Phoenix Press, London, 2000

Snyder, Louis. *Hitler and Nazism*, Franklin Watts, Inc. New York, 1961

Stein, George. *Hitler*, Prentice-Hall, Englewood Cliffs, NJ, 1968

Steinhoff, Pechel & Showalter. *Voices from The Third Reich*, Da Capro Press, NY, 1994

Sulzberger, C. L. *Picture History of World War II*, American Heritage Publishing, 1966

Sumrall, Dr. Lester. *Exorcism: The Reality of Evil*. New Leaf Press, Green Forest, AZ, 1991

Stephenson, Jill. *Women in Nazi Germany*. Pearson Education Ltd. Great Britain, 2001

Snyder, Louis. *Hitler and Nazism*, Franklin Watts, Inc. NY, 1971

Tan Books & Publishers, Inc. *The Guardian Angels*. Rockford, IL

Vance, Heidi. *Shadows Over My Berlin.* Southfarms Press, Middlehaven, CT, 1996

Waesch, Afra. *Can It Happen Again?* Angel Publishers, Monterey, CA, 1981

Waite, Robert. *Adolph Hitler, The Psychopathic God*

Walker, Thane. *I Saw Hitler Make Black Magic.* The Prosperos, El Monte, CA, 1948

Waesch, Afra. *Can It Happen Again?* Angel Press, Monterrey, CA, 1981

Whiting, Charles. *The Home Front: Germany,* Time-Life Books, Alexandria, VA, 1982

Wouk, Herman. *The Winds of War,* Pocket Books, NY, 1971

Wulff, Wilhelm. *Zodiac and Swastika,* Concord McCann, 1971

ABOUT THE AUTHOR

Master spiritual astrologer Isabel Hickey, my friend and author of the classic *Astrology, a Cosmic Science*, asked me once why I was so fascinated with Hitler and his fellow Nazis.

"I don't know," I answered, wondering the same thing.

To solve the question, Isabel regressed me into a past life incarnation when I was a male reporter in Holland. On a holiday I went to Germany. Curious about the Nazis, I attended a lecture by George Goebbels and was carried away with the Nazi philosophy.

It was difficult for me to go back to my humdrum life in Holland. Back home I got sick with pneumonia and died. After my death I immediately went in spirit back to Germany. But I became disillusioned to find that the Nazis, whom I had so admired, were only men of the lowest caliber: coarse, cruel and violent.

I found myself in that incarnation flying up into the heavens. I was in a small enclosed room, sitting on a cot. Tired and disappointed, I lay down and went to asleep. When I finally woke up, the room was full of light. A large window had opened, and I looked out over a beautiful expanse of sky. Down below the earth beckoned. Eagerly, I left the room, returned to the world, and incarnated into my present life.

Born in Gemini with the Moon in Aries, I travel wherever the wind takes me. I began studying to be a dancer at age three, and was a professional dancer for many years. At one time, similar to Afra's daughter Ellen, I did a dancing act with the USO and toured in many countries. I am certified by and taught at The First Temple of Astrology in Los Angeles. I am author of *The Star Gazer, A Hawaiian Astrological Tale, The Kahuna Way To Create The Future* and *Numerology For Personal Transformation*.

I live on Kauai with my husband Dr. Grady Deal, PhD, LMT, DC and our handsome male Pomeranian dog Sweetheart.